FIC   TAL

Tales from Grace Chapel Inn

Small-Town Reality

Carolyne Aarsen

Guideposts
CARMEL, NEW YORK

Acknowledgments

All Scripture quotations are taken from
The Holy Bible, New International Version. Copyright © 1973,
1978, 1984 International Bible Society. Used by permission
of Zondervan Bible Publishers.

www.guideposts.org
1-800-431-2344
Guideposts Books & Inspirational Media Division
Series Editors: Regina Hersey and Leo Grant
Cover art by Edgar Jerins
Cover design by Wendy Bass
Interior design by Cindy LaBreacht
Typeset by Nancy Tardi
Printed in the United States of America

Chapter  One

S o does Carlene Moss have another scintillating report in the *Acorn Nutshell* about people driving through Lancaster County?" Jane asked as Louise turned the page of the weekly newspaper on the table of the Coffee Shop.

Louise looked over the tops of her reading glasses at her younger sister, trying to read Jane's expression. Jane had a mischievous bent, which, Louise thought, should have been controlled by now. After all, at fifty years of age, a measure of maturity was called for on Jane's part.

"What do you mean?" Louise asked, hesitant to encourage her sister, but still curious.

"Oh, Acorn Hill is a quiet place," Jane said, toying with the plastic cream containers in the bowl on their table, "but surely there must be something more interesting to report than Ned Arnold's trip to Lancaster for a performance at the Fulton Opera House."

"Perhaps," Louise said, turning the page and hoping not to engage Jane in a discussion. It was obvious to Louise that Jane was in a feisty mood, and when that happened it was usually wise not to encourage her.

It was a quiet Wednesday afternoon, and the three sisters, Alice Howard, Louise Howard Smith and Jane Howard had decided to treat themselves to lunch at the local Coffee Shop instead of cooking at their home, the Grace Chapel Inn. Because they designed the inn as a bed-and-breakfast, they were not responsible for making their guests lunch or dinner, so they welcomed the chance to mingle with the residents of Acorn Hill and to be served for a change.

"Did Carlene mention anything about Clara Horn's Daisy getting loose in Viola's bookstore?" Alice asked, referring to their friend's miniature potbellied pig. "I know Clara was mortified when Daisy slipped her leash and ran free."

"I'm thankful Carlene chose to be her usual diplomatic self," Louise said with a frown. "Viola was incensed over that little pig running around her store. Not to mention what Daisy's presence did to upset Viola's cats."

"Viola's cats could do with some upsetting. Some of them are downright fat." Jane pushed aside the bowl holding the cream containers. "I know Viola is your good friend, Louise, but she spoils those cats of hers just as badly as Clara spoils that pig."

"But it is far more acceptable for a cat than a pig to be roaming free in a store."

"That's only because there aren't as many pet pigs as there are pet cats." Jane flashed Louise a playful glance. "Maybe I could help balance the equation. Maybe I should get a little pig. They are very cute."

"Our own resident feline wouldn't appreciate it," Alice put in. "Wendell gets put out enough when we get too busy. I can't imagine what kind of shenanigans that cat would get up to if you brought in a rival."

"Well, I am thankful that Carlene chose to err on the side of discretion by not printing the story." Louise turned to the next page of the paper. "It would only stir up bad feelings, and that's not good reporting."

"Sometimes I wish Carlene would do some more stirring

up," Jane said. "She makes Acorn Hill sound like a sleepy little town."

"Which is not too far off the mark," Alice put in. "We aren't exactly San Francisco, and there's nothing wrong with peace and quiet. That's what our inn customers are seeking."

Jane gave her sister an indulgent smile. "As usual, you are right, dear Alice. If I want hard-hitting news I'll have to either create it myself or find another newspaper."

"I hope you choose to find rather than create," Louise said, glancing at Jane over her glasses again.

Their waitress, Hope Collins, appeared at the table. "Are you ladies finished?"

"Yes, thank you," Louise answered, and Jane and Alice nodded their agreement.

Hope patted her hair, the color du jour an unusual coppery blond, and asked, "Isn't there anything else I can get for you? Some pie? Some ice cream? More coffee or tea?"

"I've certainly had enough." Jane handed Hope her plate. As she did, she noticed a brightly colored brochure peeking out from the pocket of Hope's apron. She tilted her head to one side as if to see it better, and Hope noticed the direction of Jane's gaze.

She patted her pocket with a proprietary air. "This is information on a cruise I want to take," she said. Then she sighed. "If I can ever get enough money together." She quickly stacked Louise's and Alice's plates on top of Jane's while she spoke.

"They are expensive," Alice agreed. "I had thought of going at one time."

"That was when your father was still alive?" Hope asked.

Alice nodded. "I couldn't leave him, and then when he passed away, Louise and Jane came home and we got the inn going and I feel like we've been busy ever since."

Jane laid a comforting hand on Alice's arm. "Louise and

I would be able to hold down the fort, I mean, inn, while you are gone. And we would even promise to play nice."

Jane and Louise loved each other dearly and usually got along well, but there were times when Jane's boisterous personality clashed with Louise's more serious one and Alice was called upon to restore peace.

Hope tugged the brochure out of her pocket with her free hand and laid it on the table in front of Alice. "If you ever think of going, this is a fantastic deal. Buffet meals, entertainment each evening, shore trips, a spa, full-time masseuse, beauty parlor with free consultations and makeovers."

It was obvious to her sisters when Alice saw the final price, because her brown eyes widened in shock.

"Wouldn't that be wonderful?" Hope's voice was filled with enthusiasm. "I've been dreaming about taking the cruise ever since a customer left this behind on her table. I would simply love to go." She then stopped and put her hand on Alice's. "Why, we could go together, Alice."

Alice unconsciously smoothed her short reddish-brown hair back from her face, buying time while she came up with a diplomatic answer. Alice would never do anything like this, but she would not want to offend Hope by saying so.

"Our Alice is a homebody at heart," Jane said, giving her sister an out. "I don't think she's given to adventures."

Alice gave her a pained look.

"Not that you're not adventurous in your own way, dear sister," Jane said, trying to cover up her unintentional insult. "I know you don't often like to leave hearth and home. You're like Beth in *Little Women*. You don't like change and are content to keep things the way they are."

They were all looking at Jane now.

"I mean, you are adaptable of course. Have to be with all the different people we have coming to the inn to stay and all those personalities you deal with at the hospital. But I mean . . ."

The gentle nudge of Louise's foot caught Jane mid-faux pas.

She glanced at Louise, whose blue eyes held a faint glint of amusement in spite of the subtle hint she was giving. Jane clamped her lips together before her words could cause any more damage.

"I'm sorry, Alice," Jane said. "My mouth was in gear, but not my brain."

Alice shrugged her comment away and added a smile for good measure. "I wasn't offended. And it's true. I like being home. That's why I stayed here in Acorn Hill while you went off to San Francisco to go to art college and Louise got married and stayed in Philadelphia. I like peace and quiet, and I certainly got that here with Father in Acorn Hill."

"Yes, but don't you ever get the urge to be somewhere else? Or be someone else?" Hope prodded, still standing by their table and holding their plates. "I know I do. That's why I accepted an invitation from a friend of mine to attend a makeup party at her place in Potterston." She looked around the table from Louise to Jane, then Alice. "Would you like to come along?"

Louise lowered her glasses and frowned her reply. "Goodness no. I don't have time for fiddling."

"Not all of us are naturally beautiful," Jane said to Louise. "Your silver hair has a natural wave, and no matter how Betty Dunkle cuts it, you always look lovely."

"Well, you certainly can't complain, Jane" Hope said. "You're so pretty yourself. No matter how I try, I can't seem to get my hair the right color or shape. I know I can use a little help."

"I don't think I'll come with you," Alice murmured, taking another sip of her tea. "But thanks for asking."

Hope picked up the brochure and tucked it into her pocket. "Oh well, I guess not all of us are cut out for trying new things."

As she left Alice sighed. "I feel as if we insulted her some-how. First the cruise, then the makeup party. It's as if we were making negative comments on her choices."

"I don't think she's that thin-skinned," Jane said. "Besides, we weren't insulting her. Just saying that the things she liked aren't for everyone. That's all."

"But still," Alice sighed, watching as Hope quickly returned to serve a new set of customers who had come in while they were talking.

"You are a dear person who cares too much at times what other people think," Louise said, patting her mouth with her napkin. "A makeup party is a waste of time and money. I don't think it's natural to color and primp."

"Oh, it's not that bad," Jane said, twirling a strand of long dark hair around her finger. "It's no different from dressing up and wearing nice clothes."

Louise couldn't think of a suitable reply to her youngest sister's comment and chose to change the subject. "We should be getting back to the inn. I have some correspon-dence to deal with, and I want to finish reading the *Acorn Nutshell* in the peace and quiet of our home."

"Our home, sweet home," Alice said as they got up. "And I have to get ready for my ANGELs meeting this evening."

"What project do you have planned for your girls this week?" Jane asked as she paid for their meals.

"This week is a craft week. I'm not sure what special project I will have them do for this month."

Alice was the leader of a church group of middle-school girls called the ANGELs. They met once a week for Bible Study and crafts. Also, to help teach the girls the value of giv-ing without receiving, Alice had the girls do monthly anony-mous acts of kindness.

"The girls enjoyed the Rake and Run we did earlier last fall," Alice said. "I know some of the older people were grate-ful that we cleaned their yards."

"Clara Horn mentioned something to me just the other day," Louise said as they left the Coffee Shop. "She asked me to pass on her thanks. She was so happy she didn't have to rake leaves last fall."

"I thought she had some boys do her raking last fall," Jane said.

"She did," Alice said, "but leaves from her neighbors' trees blew onto her property afterward. I'm amazed she still tries to keep that large yard up. It's a lot of work for an older woman on her own."

"It's her home," Louise said. "And as Father always said, 'Old trees don't transplant that well.' For Clara Horn, the situation is most likely the same."

"I don't blame her," Jane said. "I can't imagine not having a garden or a yard to work on." Jane drew in a long, slow breath of the brisk air. "Ah, spring. Things are new and fresh. You can almost hear the plants growing."

"How many pumpkins are you going to plant this year?" Louise asked, a teasing note in her voice.

"About one third of what I did last year." Jane shook her head, remembering the bounty of her pumpkin crop. "The other day I found a container buried in the bottom of the freezer that held pumpkin muffins I made last fall."

"Our guests certainly enjoyed the abundance," Alice said as they went up the walk to the inn. "And Lloyd was a big hit when he brought those extra muffins to the town hall meeting that one day."

"Speaking of town hall meeting, are either of you going?" Jane asked.

"I hope to," Alice said. "I don't have to work at the hospital that day, and I'm eager to see what the council will do about some of the items on the agenda that was in the *Nutshell*."

Louise held the back door to the inn open for her sisters. "Yes, some of those proposals sound interesting."

"I'm going out back to check over the garden," Jane said. "I'll join you and Louise later."

"You were just out there this morning," Alice said to Jane. "What could possibly have changed?"

Jane gave Alice an indulgent smile. "Spoken like a true nongardener," she said. "I'm just going to putter around. Pull a few weeds. Talk to my plants."

"You go putter, and I'll get to my correspondence," Louise said as she exited the kitchen into the hall.

Jane was just about to go out to the porch to gather her gardening gloves and basket, when the kitchen door opened and her aunt bustled in.

Though the weather was warm, Ethel wore a bright-pink knit hat pulled tightly over her head. Her pale blue eyes were wide with what seemed to be a combination of shock and grief.

"What am I going to do?" she wailed, clutching Jane's arm. "I'll never be able to go out in public again."

Jane glanced over her aunt's head to Alice, who lifted her hands in a puzzled gesture.

"Why won't you be able to go out again? What happened?" Jane asked, curious but not too concerned. Their aunt was a dear person with a flair for the dramatic, and Jane guessed that right now that flair was being exercised.

"I wanted to try something different," Ethel said, sniffing softly as she eased herself onto a nearby chair, pressing the palms of her hands against her cotton skirt. "I didn't want to look old."

Ethel lived in the carriage house just behind Grace Chapel Inn, and though the sisters were privy to most parts of their aunt's life, her age was the one thing she didn't discuss with them. While she claimed to be younger than seventy, the sisters were sure she was older.

"I didn't want to look like Martha Bevins, Clara Horn and Florence Simpson. I wanted something different."

"More different than bright red hair?" Jane asked.

"Different than I always look. Betty Dunkle offered to do some streaks for me, but I thought that would cost too much. I have to watch my pennies you know. Well, nickels too. These days pennies don't count for much. I still save them. Have a bucket full of them. I should roll them and bring them into the bank some day. But I did use my saved-up quarters to buy myself one of those home-streaking kits and tried to do it on my own."

"And how did it turn out?" Jane asked, though the hat offered a clue.

Ethel let her shoulders slump and slowly pulled off the stocking cap.

Jane immediately pressed her lips together, and Alice lifted her hand to her mouth.

Ethel's deep-red hair was now lined with frizzy baby-pink stripes of varying widths.

She looked like a mashed candy cane.

"Well . . ." Jane said, drawing the word out as she struggled to find something diplomatic to say. "If different was what you were going for, you got there."

"I know," Ethel wailed, dropping her pink and red head into her hands. "I look like a member of one of those pink rock bands."

Jane shot Alice a puzzled look. "Pink rock band?"

"You know," Ethel cried in frustration. "The ones with all the earrings and goofy hair color and ripped clothes."

"Oh. Punk rock."

"That's what I said."

Alice sat beside her aunt and laid a consoling hand on her shoulder. "What exactly did you do?"

"I just wanted some streaks. When I was done I thought they looked a little odd. So I washed my hair, which made it go funny, so I thought I would try to lighten the color up a bit with another box of hair color and then"—she pointed to her head—"I got this. Then I thought if I permed my bangs I might distract people from the pink. I know I should have gone to Betty right away, but I felt so silly. Now I've gone from bad to worse."

"I don't know much about color or permanents, but I'm guessing that you really can't do anything until your hair grows out a bit and you can have it trimmed," Jane said. "You may just have to live with it until Betty can fix it."

"I finally worked up the nerve to phone Betty, but she said that she can't do anything for me. She said that she didn't have the expertise."

"What about Potterston? Surely there's someone there you can see," Alice said.

"I tried several shops, but the earliest opening I could get as a new customer was in three weeks, and I can't go out looking like this."

"Do you really care so much what other people think?" Alice asked.

Ethel looked from Jane to Alice and then sighed dramatically. "I know I shouldn't care, but this is just too much even for me to tough out." She dropped her chin into her hands, then suddenly sat up. "Oh my goodness. Whatever will Lloyd think?"

Jane had to stop herself from laughing again. She had to confess that she had wondered what Lloyd Tynan, Ethel's beau and the mayor of Acorn Hill, would have to say about Ethel's do-it-yourself beautification project. Lloyd didn't appreciate change simply for change's sake. He liked his life and Acorn Hill the way it was and often told people that.

"I'm sure he'll understand," Jane said

"We were supposed to go out for dinner to Potterston tomorrow." Ethel sighed heavily. "I can't now. Not looking like this." She ran her fingers through her locks as if to make sure what she had was still there. "What shall I do?"

"Wear a wig?" Jane said, half-jokingly.

"I might have to."

The front doorbell rang, sending Ethel to her feet. "You have guests. I can't let them see me like this." She tugged her cap over her head and with a quick wave to her nieces, scampered out the back door.

Jane looked at Alice and they both started laughing.

"Dear Aunt Ethel," Alice said when she got her breath back again. "She continues to surprise me."

Chapter Two

"Welcome to Acorn Hill and to Grace Chapel Inn, Mr. Swigart," Louise said when their latest guest had finished signing in.

"Please, call me Woody," Elwood Swigart said. "After all, I'm going to be a permanent resident of the town as soon as I can move into my new home."

He was a tall, imposing man with dark eyebrows and piercing gray eyes. His neatly trimmed beard gave him an air of distinction that softened the harsh planes of his face. He wore a soft-green cardigan sweater over a white shirt teamed with relaxed camel-colored wool pants. Elegant, but not showy.

He picked up his suitcase and looked around the entry hall, one hand lightly fingering his beard. "I understand this inn used to be your home and that your father was a minister in the chapel just beside this place."

"Grace Chapel Inn is still our home," Louise said as she led him up the stairs to the first floor. "My sisters and I live on the floor above this one." She opened the door of the Garden Room and gave it a quick glance. All was in order, as it should be, but it never hurt to double-check. "This is your room," she said as he strode in, inspecting it for himself.

He dropped one suitcase onto the floor and carefully laid his worn and battered briefcase on the rosewood bureau. He moved to the window, swept the white gauze curtain aside and looked out at the garden.

Over his shoulder, Louise could see Jane gently tugging weeds out of the dirt.

"Is that one of your sisters down below?"

"Yes. Jane. She does most of our cooking. She used to be a chef in San Francisco."

"And your other sister, Alice, she lived here all her life? With your father?" Woody asked as he turned away from the window.

Louise couldn't stop the frown lines that formed on her forehead. "I'm sorry, how do you know so much about us?"

He snapped open his briefcase and pulled out some notebooks. "I make it my business to know as much as I can about a place before I move in." He gave her a quick smile. "Occupational hazard. I used to be a newspaper editor in Pittsburgh. And I discovered that the people in this town are very forthcoming in their information."

"We are a friendly town," Louise agreed.

He took a copy of the *Acorn Nutshell* from his briefcase. "I gather this is the local rag?"

"That is our newspaper," Louise agreed, trying not to bristle at his terminology.

He nodded. "Pretty tame stuff. What is the editor covering up?"

"This is a tame town," Louise said. "There is nothing to hide. What you see is what you get in Acorn Hill."

Woody stroked his beard as if pondering Louise's remark. "If there's one thing I've discovered in my years as an editor and reporter, there is no such thing as nothing to hide," he said. "Every town, no matter how big or small, has its secrets."

"I have no doubts that there are secrets in Acorn Hill, but I suspect that none of them is interesting." Louise said this all with a smile, but underneath her calm demeanor she felt a tick of unease. It was as if Woody wanted to find something wrong with their town. "I hope you enjoy your stay with us," she said.

"I hope so too."

As Louise was turning to leave, Woody called her name.

"I was wondering about staying here longer than the ten days I had booked, in case the carpenters working on the house aren't finished on time."

Louise thought a moment, then shook her head. "I'm sorry. I don't believe we have any vacancies."

"So you would put me on the street?" Woody asked.

Louise caught a peculiar tone in his voice and then, as she met his gray eyes, she saw an unfamiliar glint.

Was he taunting her?

"I don't imagine it would come to that, Mr. Swigart," Louise said lightly.

"Please, I'm going to be a neighbor. I would prefer you call me Woody."

"I hope you enjoy your introduction to Acorn Hill via our inn, Woody." Louise gave him a polite smile and then left. As she walked back down the stairs to the desk in the reception area, she hoped that his house would be done on time. She would feel terrible if she did, indeed, have to ask him to vacate his room, but the inn was fully booked this month, and there was nothing she could do about it.

"I am so glad you decided to come with me to this makeup party," Hope said to Alice as she drove toward Potterston Thursday evening. "I was told I get a special gift if I bring a friend."

"That's a good incentive," Alice agreed. When Hope first

asked Alice to accompany her to the makeup party, Alice's thoughts on the activity reflected those of Louise. She knew that her looks didn't define her and that God looked at the heart, which was more important than outward appearance. But somehow Jane's comments about her being a homebody, innocent as they were, had touched a sore spot.

When Jane and Louise had left Acorn Hill to go their own ways, Alice faithfully stayed behind, happily single, taking care of their father, Rev. Daniel Howard. Her work at the hospital as a nurse was fulfilling, as was her work with the young people of Grace Chapel.

When her father died, her sisters returned, and it seemed that her life turned a corner. They started the inn and were reasonably successful. She and her sisters got along and had wonderful times together. They had their disagreements, but on the whole, their lives puttered along without trouble.

Yet in spite of her basic contentment, Alice couldn't forget Jane's latest comments.

Jane drew attention everywhere she went. Though she was middle-aged, she dressed and acted like a much younger person. Jane's motto was that age is just a number, and she lived according to that idea. Her flamboyant clothes and easygoing manner drew a variety of people, and though Alice was never jealous, at times she wished she had Jane's self-confidence.

Louise was possessed of a quiet self-confidence. She had taught music all her life, was independent by nature and was not easily influenced by people or opinions.

Alice knew herself to be a typical middle child. She was a peacemaker. She wanted everyone to get along and wanted things to go smoothly.

Of course, Alice stood up for principles and tried to make a difference. Her work as a ward nurse in Potterston Hospital had its moments of drama, but generally her job was to care for other people.

Overall, Jane was right. Alice often *was* thinking of other people. She didn't spend much time on herself.

So on the spur of the moment, after thinking all of this over, she called Hope and asked if she could come to the party after all.

"Have you ever been to a makeup party before?" Hope asked as she drove into Potterston.

"This would be my first time."

"Mine too," Hope said. "I've been to a few of those other home parties. You know—the kind where they sell plasticware and candles and such, but never makeup. I think this party could be a lot of fun."

Alice hoped so. When she told Louise and Jane that she was going, both looked puzzled. Well, that was good. For once she hadn't been predictable.

Hope glanced at a piece of paper she was holding, then at the name of the street they were approaching. "I think this is the place."

She turned onto the street and parked behind a row of cars.

"Looks like there are a lot of women here already," Hope said as they walked up the sidewalk to the house.

The house fairly buzzed with women laughing and chatting with each other. Alice didn't know anyone but Hope, and for a moment, she regretted coming and wished she were back home.

That's just silly. I'm here now and enjoying a new adventure.

Hope introduced her to the hostess, Marty Anderson. She was a young woman with the kind of peaches-and-cream complexion that didn't need any enhancement. Alice wondered why she was holding a makeup party.

"Welcome to my Beauty Bound party. Help yourself to coffee or tea from the table along the wall," Marty said, smiling in welcome. "I have some goodies there as well." Then she gestured to the tall, dark-haired woman standing beside her. "This is Dominique Bartell. She is our Beauty Bound consultant for the evening."

Dominique's sage-green linen suit was simple and elegant, and its color complemented her coffee-colored skin perfectly. Her soft-brown eyes were enhanced with shimmering pale-green shadow. She was the epitome of style.

"Welcome," Dominique said. "Have either of you ever been to a Beauty Bound presentation before?" Her well-modulated voice had the barest hint of an English accent.

"This is my first," Hope gushed, looking around at the group of assembled ladies. "I'm excited to see what this is all about."

"And I'm excited to help you bring out your natural beauty," Dominique handed each of them a catalog with what looked to be an order form discreetly tucked in. "Have a seat. We'll begin as soon as all the ladies have arrived."

Alice and Hope found an empty table. In the center was a tray filled with tubes and tiny cases. At each place lay a soft-blue paper mat with a fold-up mirror.

"I guess we're going to be doing this hands-on," Hope said, pulling her chair closer to the table, her eyes bright with anticipation.

Another group of women came in, also laughing and chattering, and Alice felt a flicker of relief mixed with surprise when she heard a familiar voice. She turned to see her aunt, who wore a tight-fitting cloche that covered her hair completely.

After Ethel got her catalog she spied Alice and Hope and hurried over.

"I certainly didn't think to find you here," she said to Alice as she pulled her chair close to the table. "This will be such fun."

"I like the hat, Aunt Ethel," Alice said.

Ethel put a hand self-consciously to her head, adjusting the hat, then glanced around. She saw that Hope was engrossed in her catalog and that Clara Horn, with whom she had come, was still making her way toward the table. She leaned close to Alice and said in a whisper, "I really wanted to come tonight. So I dug through the attic and found this. I'm letting people think that I'm going for a signature look by wearing hats everywhere."

"You look lovely, Aunt," Alice told her.

Clara, who had just arrived at the table, chimed in, "I think it looks so stylish. I believe I might want to start wearing hats again."

Ethel gave Alice a conspiratorial wink, then turned her attention to the catalog and soon was busy narrating it to Alice, Clara and Hope, though each had her own.

"Oh my goodness, look at what they're charging for a tube of mascara," Ethel exclaimed, shaking her head. "I heard this product was expensive, but I didn't expect these prices."

Alice glanced at her own catalog and had to catch herself from saying almost the same thing. The prices were far higher than she had expected. She didn't know if she could justify buying anything here tonight, but at the same time she had come to the house of a woman she had never met. She felt obligated to purchase something.

Marty Anderson called for everyone's attention and introduced Dominique again.

Dominique gave a brief rundown of how Beauty Bound started and where the products were made. She spoke of how she made a living selling these beauty aids and how much she enjoyed her job and the freedom it gave her. She encouraged all the women present to consider a career with Beauty Bound and said she would be happy to help any woman who was interested in achieving financial independence.

Alice listened politely, wondering what this all had to do with wearing makeup. After a bit more about the benefits and perks of working for Beauty Bound, Dominique pointed out the specials for the evening and the advantages of being a hostess. After some explanation of what Marty would be receiving for hosting this event, Dominique finally drew their attention to the tray of cosmetics on the table.

She sat Marty down and first demonstrated the skin-cleansing portion of the product line, then the makeup. When she was done, she encouraged each of the women to try out the products on her table.

Soon the noise level increased. Women were opening tubes and pots and smearing and brushing and laughing. Alice couldn't help but get caught up in the spirit of the evening and soon was applying makeup with abandon.

"If you don't like what you have done, you can remove the makeup with the cotton pads in the bowl in front of you, making sure to use the Beauty Bound eye-makeup remover," Dominique informed the group of chattering women.

"Here, Alice, try this color," Ethel said, handing her a pot of green eye shadow. It looked to be the same sage color that Dominique was wearing. "This will look lovely with your brown eyes. I can't wear green like that. Especially not now," Ethel said. Then, realizing her mistake, she quickly looked at Hope and Clara to see if they had heard her comment. They were both busy with their makeup.

Dominique stopped by their table to give them a few hints and to point out some of the other products in the catalog.

"I gather all you ladies are from the same town," she said, glancing around the table.

"We all call Acorn Hill home," Ethel said proudly.

"Oh, I just visited Acorn Hill. It is a lovely town." Dominique pulled up an empty chair and sat at the table with them. "I suppose there are a number of women in Acorn Hill, single and married?" she asked.

"Oh my, yes," Ethel said, picking up a tube of mascara. "We don't just have men you know."

"I'm sorry, that sounded wrong." Dominique's laugh was rich and warm. "The reason I'm asking is that I've been throwing around ideas for a new reality television show with a producer friend of mine." She glanced around the table expectantly. "One of the ideas I had was to work with women of a variety of ages in a small town. Show viewers that not all makeovers have to involve fancy stylists and expensive makeup. That many of them can be done right where they live."

"A makeover show?" Ethel asked, unconsciously fingering her hat. "In our small town? Who would be in charge?"

"That would probably be Noralee Spracht. She is a producer of KPMY Television and has been looking for precisely the right venue for this production. I think your little town might be perfect." Dominique's excited brown eyes glanced from one lady to the other. "Do you think women of Acorn Hill would be amenable to something like this?"

"A-mean-a-what?" Clara Horn asked, glancing from Alice to Ethel.

"Dominique is asking us if women in Acorn Hill would participate if a television crew came to town to do a makeover show," Alice gently explained.

"I think that could be fun," Hope said. "I always like reading about makeovers in women's magazines."

"I don't know if that's such a good idea," Clara said. "I mean, putting on makeup for fun is one thing, but doing it on television is another thing completely."

Dominique held up her hand in a placating gesture. "Noralee is the soul of discretion."

"I think it's a marvelous idea," Ethel said decisively. "I'm sure that we could convince people to participate."

Dominique smiled. "This is wonderful. I know you ladies would enjoy this immensely. I'll contact her as soon as possible."

"Would such a show be disruptive to the town?" Alice asked.

Dominique shook her head. "Reality shows work with what is available, so there isn't much disruption. Noralee told me that such a reality show would require only a couple of cameramen, a commentator and a few assistants."

Ethel fingered her hat, contemplative. Alice would have given anything to know what was clicking behind her pale blue eyes.

"Think about it," Dominique said as she got up. Before she returned to her duties as a hostess, she rested her hand lightly on Ethel's shoulder, singling her out. "I'll put Noralee in touch with you."

She left and Hope leaned forward. "This sounds so exciting. A television show in our town."

"There's nothing settled yet, Hope," Alice gently reminded her. "She is just asking around."

Hope looked like she was about to say more, but just then Marty brought out trays of food and the conversation ended.

Half an hour later, the party was winding down, and Dominique was at the front taking orders. Alice had paged through the catalog a number of times and finally decided on a tube of hand cream that wasn't as expensive as some of the other items.

When she brought her order to the front, Dominique was friendly and asked her to sit down while she wrote out her order. She asked Alice questions about the party, about the product. Did she like it? Was she excited about it? Would she like to get some of her own at a much reduced rate?

Alice understood that Dominique was hoping that she would be willing to host a party and gently told her that all she was interested in today was the cream. Dominique gave her a gracious smile and adroitly moved on to Alice's order.

Alice paid and then got up to make room for Hope, who was one of the last to finalize her choices.

Alice caught Ethel standing by the food table. She and Clara were huddled together talking but stopped when Alice joined them.

"Did you try some of Marty's apple tart?" Ethel said, holding out a plate to Alice.

"I did. It was delicious," Alice said. "Ethel, I was—"

"Of course, her tarts are not as good as Jane's, but then Marty didn't work at a fancy restaurant either," Ethel said, delicately wiping away the crumbs from her mouth.

"Aunt Ethel, I want to talk to you about the television show."

Ethel looked up at Alice, her expression innocent. "What about the television show?"

"I think that you should wait until there is something definite on the table before you spread the news about the show."

"Why, dear, you talk as if I were a gossip," Ethel said, with a smile.

Alice knew that Ethel's network of communication in Acorn Hill would put Interpol to shame. If she put out the word, it would spread of its own accord. And if Ethel added that she wanted this to happen, the chances were good that they would.

However, Ethel was being coy, so Alice let the topic drop.

On the way home, Hope chatted about what Dominique had told them. "What do you think, Alice? Do you think that a reality show is a good idea?"

"I don't have a huge problem with it," Alice said. "As long as the show doesn't cause a disruption."

"From what Dominique said, it didn't sound like the show would." Hope pulled into the driveway of the inn and came to a stop. "I'm glad you came along tonight," she said to Alice. "Did you have a good time?"

"Yes I did. The party was fun."

Alice said good-bye and closed the door of the car. She watched as Hope backed down the driveway. Then Alice turned back to the inn. The windows of the living room glowed welcomingly.

She smiled. Returning to the inn in the daytime didn't give her the same sense of homecoming that arriving in the evening did. Whenever she came back from an evening shift at the hospital and the lights were on in the inn, she had the same sense of expectation.

Maybe Jane was right about her, Alice thought with a chuckle as she let herself in. Maybe she was just a homebody after all.

Chapter Three

Jane stacked her hands over the top of the rake handle and rested her chin on her fingers as the warm afternoon sun beat on her head. She looked over the garden like a general surveying troops. This Saturday afternoon had been productive. She battled with nature and won.

For now.

A seasoned gardener like Jane knew better than to rejoice in the momentary victory of woman over weeds. She knew that even now, pernicious little leaves were pushing themselves to the surface, ready to make a mockery of her rows of vegetables that were just starting to show themselves.

"I'll be back," she warned with a deep voice, mimicking the famous words of an action-hero movie star.

She turned to put her rake away and faced Woody Swigart, who had been watching her, his hands tucked in the pockets of his neatly pressed khaki pants.

"General knowledge seems to be that talking gently to plants encourages growth. Gardeners must do things differently down here," he said, smiling at her.

"I was actually addressing the weeds," Jane said, gesturing toward the pile she had yet to gather up. "The curse on the earth."

"Ah. Genesis. When Adam is turned out of the garden." He gave her another smile. "You look surprised. You didn't think that an old newshound would know much about the Bible?"

Jane lifted her shoulders in a shrug. "I have to admit that I had you in a different cubbyhole."

"Ah, I'm not that easily categorized."

Jane heard the warning as much in his tone as in his words. "I think categorizing people is an occupational hazard," she said, "but I will admit that my snap decisions have had to be unsnapped from time to time."

"At any rate, I didn't come here to discuss theology or gardening. I don't think the former is uplifting or necessary and the latter is a waste of time. I was wondering about the town council meetings. When are they generally held?"

Jane had to push down a rising resentment at how easily he dismissed both her faith and her avocation. As innkeepers, she and her sisters often faced people who didn't hold the same beliefs they did, but they had also learned not to let personal feelings interfere with their guests' comfort.

She and her sisters firmly believed that they were to be Christ's representatives on earth. Hospitality was their chosen tool. At times that meant ignoring comments and learning to appreciate a variety of personalities.

Jane had to think a moment. "I believe on Monday at town hall. In the morning."

"Are they open to the public?"

"They are, though few people attend."

"Is the interest level low?" he asked.

"Maybe the trust level is high," she answered with a smile. "We tend to let our mayor take charge of things, Mr. Swigart."

"That's a dangerous tendency," he said. "And please, call me Woody."

"Okay, Woody," she said. "Why is that dangerous?" She

poked at an errant weed that she had missed with one of the tines of her rake. She had a sense that Woody was feeling her out about the new place where he had decided to settle. She had time, so she meandered over to the bench that Fred Humbert had helped her install. She and her sisters often sat here to enjoy the garden.

He followed her lead and sat beside her.

"People must be involved in their town life," he was saying. "You can't let someone else take charge without accountability. An uninvolved populace risks being run by an autocracy."

Jane had to smile at the thought of Lloyd Tynan as an autocrat. Sure he had a tendency to be bombastic, but Lloyd was dedicated and sensitive to the needs of the community.

If Woody was going to be a permanent resident in the town, he ought to know how things worked here. "We know our mayor and the town council quite well," she said, leaning back on the bench, tapping the ground lightly with her rake as she spoke. "They all live in the town with us. Most of them work here. They drink coffee in the Coffee Shop and occasionally have a treat at the Good Apple. We see them on the street and, if people have something that bothers them, the issue usually gets dealt with face-to-face."

"But the meetings are where the decisions are made."

Jane nodded absently, watching the flight of a butterfly as it flitted past them. "You'll have to indulge my curiosity," she said. "Why are you interested in the meetings?"

Woody looked away. "I'm just a concerned citizen," he said. Then he pushed himself off the bench. "And I've taken up a lot of your time. I had better make sure that things are progressing on my house according to schedule. I do want to have a place to move into when my time is up here." He gave her a careful smile, then left.

Jane stayed on the bench a moment longer, enjoying the warm sun but also puzzling over Woody's expressed concern about the town council meetings. And his evasive answer to her question.

But she didn't puzzle too long. Life was too short to get involved in the peculiarities of their guests.

Instead, she leaned back on the bench and drew in a long, slow breath, savoring the vague scent of lilacs blooming. The smell teased out older memories of spring in Acorn Hill. How light and free she always felt in the spring when winter coats were shed and heavy boots were replaced with light-as-a-feather sneakers. How the runoff from the melting snow would flow in the street gutters, and how she and her friends would sail paper boats in the small streams of water that followed the curbs, getting encouragement and advice from passersby.

Happy memories, she thought, pushing herself off the bench. *Acorn Hill is a good place to have grown up and to live.*

"That woman, Clara Horn, does she really carry a pot-bellied pig in that buggy she pushes around town?" Woody helped himself to another Belgian waffle and mounded a generous helping of glazed peaches over the top. It was Tuesday morning at the inn. Their other guests were still sleeping, but Woody was up early. Because he was by himself, Alice, Louise and Jane had invited him to join them for breakfast in the kitchen.

"That pig is like a child to her," Alice said as she refilled his cup with coffee.

"I'm surprised that the town council hasn't put a bylaw in place about exotic pets on the loose." Woody frowned as he added a dollop of whipped cream to his waffle. "It has to be extremely unhealthy."

"Actually, I think dear Daisy is a picture of health," Jane said, deliberately misunderstanding him.

Woody shot her an annoyed glance from under his bristling eyebrows, but Jane simply smiled at him innocently.

"I'm sure that I'm not the only person in this town who objects to that woman pushing around a pig in a buggy."

Jane immediately thought of how upset Viola was when Daisy got loose in her bookstore. But she wasn't about to give Woody any ammunition. Something about him told her to keep up her guard. "Oh," she responded, "she doesn't always do that. Sometimes she walks Daisy on a leash."

"I did mention the pig to a few other people around town, but they seem to take it as casually as you do, Jane," Woody said, his turned-down mouth expressing his objections.

"We are a fairly open-minded group," Jane said.

"Having a pig for a pet is no different, I would presume, than having a cat or a dog." Louise patted her mouth delicately with her napkin.

Jane was mildly surprised at Louise's quiet defense of Clara and her pig. There was a time when Louise would have agreed with Woody.

"But dogs or cats are required to be licensed in most municipalities," Woody said. He took a quick bite of his waffle as he glanced around the table. "I'm surprised that Acorn Hill isn't as forward-looking."

"Our dogs are required to be licensed," Jane replied.

Woody said nothing, but Jane could see that he wasn't convinced. Jane was about to add something when Louise cleared her throat.

"How is the work on your house coming?" Louise asked, diplomatically bringing the conversation back to something less controversial.

"It's coming along better than I expected," he said. He took a sip of his coffee, and Jane was surprised to see the hint of a smile behind that beard. "This meal is excellent and the coffee is some of the best I've had."

"Jane is a wonderful cook," Alice agreed. "We're blessed to have her." Alice's compliment restored Jane's good mood. Trust Alice to find exactly the right thing to say.

Woody raised his cup to Jane as if toasting her. He looked as if he was about to say something, but the back door opened and Ethel entered the kitchen, breathless.

"Such news. Such news." Ethel sat down on the nearest empty chair, fanning herself with a copy of the newspaper. Today she wore a natural straw hat with her hair tucked carefully under it and out of sight. Ethel turned to Woody, her smile bright and welcoming. "I'm Ethel Buckley. I am the girls' aunt." She reached across the table to shake his hand.

"Woody Swigart." He gave her a gracious nod as he took her hand. "You certainly don't look old enough to be their aunt," he said.

What a smoothie, Jane thought, almost rolling her eyes.

Ethel lowered her eyes as a faint blush crept up her neck. "Well, I was a half sister to Daniel Howard, who was Louise, Jane and Alice's father. I was born later than he was. Much, much later."

"And you live around here?"

"In the carriage house," she said, waving her hand vaguely, "behind here."

"What brings you here, Aunt Ethel?" Jane said, "You look as if you are on a mission."

"I've got news," Ethel said.

"We've already read that issue of the *Acorn Nutshell,* Auntie," Jane said, pointing to the paper Ethel was using as a fan.

Ethel gave her a puzzled glance, then looked at the paper she was holding. "No. Oh my, no, the news isn't in here. This is last week's paper and of course there's nothing new in here for you. Although I was interested to note that Nia Komonos is going to be bringing some new books into the library. And it looks like a really interesting variety. I might even have to pick some up. Not that I do much reading, mind you. I don't always have the time."

Jane pressed her lips together to hold back a smile. Their aunt often seemed to have too much time on her hands.

"But if this Noralee lady comes to stay here, then we are going to be busy, busy."

Louise gave her aunt a puzzled look. "What Noralee lady? I don't believe we have anyone of that name down for reservations."

"Well, she might be calling. Of course, I know you are booked up at the inn here, so she might have to stay somewhere else, but I'm sure she could find a place. I can't believe she's actually going to come."

"Are you talking about Noralee Spracht? The television producer that Dominique was telling us about?" Alice asked.

Ethel nodded, looking satisfied with herself. "She called me just now."

"I'm sorry to interrupt you, Aunt Ethel," Jane said, getting up. "But would you like some breakfast?"

Ethel's bright eyes flitted over the table. "Waffles? Oh my, yes, I love your waffles, Jane."

Jane quickly brought her a plate and some extra cutlery. Louise had already poured their aunt a cup of coffee and in a matter of seconds, Ethel was tucking in. She closed her eyes and sighed lightly. "Jane, you have outdone yourself again. These waffles are divine."

"Why would a television producer be coming here to Acorn Hill?" Jane asked.

"To do the *Changing Faces* makeover reality program," Ethel said.

"I beg your pardon?" Louise asked.

"*Changing Faces?*" Jane asked with a lift of her eyebrows. "That sounds like a witness-protection program."

"Surely a television producer can't simply come traipsing into town and start filming," Louise said.

"Oh no. They need to talk to the town council first," Ethel said. "But I'm sure they won't have any problems. Especially if I tell Lloyd I think the program would be a good idea."

"I take it you are talking about your mayor?" Woody asked.

"Ethel is good friends with Mayor Tynan," Jane said by way of explanation.

"And that's all it takes to have something you want happen in Acorn Hill? Be friends with the mayor?"

Too late Jane realized how that sounded, especially to someone like Woody, who seemed determined to find something wrong with their town council and how it conducted business.

"Well, it doesn't hurt," Ethel said with a wink.

Jane almost groaned. Ethel's innocent comments would only add to the false perception of Acorn Hill forming in Woody's mind.

"You were telling us about Noralee?" Alice said. "Is she really going to come here?"

"What does she want to do?" Louise asked.

"You know those reality shows? Where they follow people around and film them? Then show the program later?" Ethel asked, warming to the subject. "This Noralee woman wants to do the same here in Acorn Hill, but she wants to film makeovers."

"Are you talking makeup and hairstyles and the like?" Louise asked.

"Yes. They will give you advice on how to do your hair and how to dress and what kind of makeup would best suit you. A complete makeover. I talked to her this morning and she wants to come tomorrow."

"I think the notion is ridiculous," Louise said, emphasizing the point with one raised brow. "It's not right to spend so much time on primping and fussing about your looks. What's worse is having people all over the county see you make a fool of yourself." She shook her head as if dismissing the show, the producer and the entire idea. "What's wrong with accepting yourself the way God made you?"

"A strong sense of self is a gift that not everyone has," Alice said, gently toning down her sister's comments. "However, I don't think Woody is interested in talking about this subject."

"Oh, on the contrary, I am fascinated." He leaned forward, his posture underlining his interest.

Jane studied him, trying to understand why he would be interested. But she got no hint from his expression.

"Do you know when she will be coming?" Woody asked Ethel.

Ethel shook her head. "I have to talk to Lloyd about putting the proposal on the town council agenda and then get back to her." She sat back with a satisfied sigh. "I think this could be a lot of fun."

"Telling a woman she needs to improve herself can be demeaning." Louise set her coffee cup down and pushed herself away from the table, signaling the end of the discussion for her.

"There's nothing demeaning about wanting to look nice," Ethel said, tugging on her hat and lifting her chin. "And I'm going to tell Lloyd to make sure they let this happen." She got up as well.

"You didn't finish your breakfast," Jane said. Ethel must be quite upset not to eat the rest of her waffles.

"I have things to do. Louise might not think this is a good idea, but then Louise isn't always right." She gave an extra tug on her hat, then swept out of the kitchen with as much grace as her short, slightly plump body would allow.

A moment of silence followed Ethel's departure. Jane could tell that Ethel was miffed with Louise, but she also knew that, given time, she would come around. Ethel was not one to hold grudges.

"Your aunt left her newspaper behind," Woody said, picking it off the table.

"I'm sure she's already read the paper front to back," Jane said, "but I'll make sure she gets it."

He glanced at the paper and shook his head. "I can't believe that this passes for front-page news in this town." He held up the paper, showing Alice and Jane what they had already seen: a picture of a group of smiling school children holding up some wildflowers they had picked on a field trip.

Behind them was the smiling face of their teacher, Vera Humbert, Alice's good friend and walking partner.

"It's a general-interest story."

"I'm not interested, and I'm sure other people would find the story dull. I'm sure there are other things going on in this town that deserve some reporting." Woody frowned, then put the paper down.

"We don't have a lot of closets with skeletons here," Jane said quietly, puzzled that he should be so negative about what Carlene reported on. In fact, Woody seemed opinionated about the ordinary things that happened in Acorn Hill.

She wondered why.

Alice interrupted her thoughts. "Oh my, look at the time. I'm sorry to eat and run, Jane, but I have to get ready for work."

"I thought this bed-and-breakfast was your occupation," Woody said.

"I work part-time as a nurse at Potterston Hospital," Alice told him as she carried her plate and utensils to the counter.

"That's commendable," Woody said.

"I truly enjoy the work, as I enjoy the work here," Alice said. She gave him a quick smile and left the room before he could ask her any more questions.

Chapter Four

J ane, this is Sasha Webber, our newest guest," Louise said as Jane entered the front hall Wednesday afternoon. Louise stood behind the desk that was tucked under the stairs. She was writing out a receipt for a young woman who wore a plain brown shirt and pants. She had one small suitcase on the floor next to her. "Ms. Webber, this is my sister Jane Howard. She is also part-owner of the inn and is our chef."

Sasha had thick, copper-colored hair that was braided in a shiny plait that hung halfway down her back. She had brown eyes, but Jane only caught a glimpse of them, because Sasha looked down as soon as Louise introduced them.

"Welcome to our inn," Jane said, shaking her hand, "and welcome to Acorn Hill."

"Ms. Webber is the winner of the passport contest that ran in Potterston last fall," Louise told her.

Jane recalled that a group of businesses in Potterston, eager to draw awareness to the area, had run a contest encouraging people to tour the county with a pretend passport and enter drawings at each stop. Various businesses participated, and one of the prizes was a two-week stay at Grace Chapel Inn. The group coordinating the contest purchased the stay.

"Congratulations," Jane said. "I'm glad you won."

"I wouldn't have even entered the contest if it wasn't for my friend," Sasha said, giving Jane a shy smile. "She took me along to some of the places and made me enter the drawings. It's amazing that I won. I . . . I never travel much or get out much and here I am . . ." she paused and looked around. "Here, in this beautiful inn. In the inn. That's kind of funny, don't you think?"

"It is kind of funny, and I hope you enjoy your prize, in the inn." Sasha seemed like a sweet young woman, and Jane was already taken with her.

"Jane, would you be so kind as to show Ms. Webber to her room?" Louise asked. "I have a music student coming in five minutes."

"You teach music here?" Sasha asked, picking up her suitcase and following Jane up the stairs.

"Don't worry," Jane told her. "You won't be disturbed by the noise. Louise teaches in the parlor, which is soundproofed."

"The sound of the music wouldn't disturb me," Sasha said, brushing Jane's assurances away with a quick wave of her hand. "I'm pretty easygoing that way. I don't get disturbed much at all." Sasha had a light, breathy voice that seemed at odds with her no-nonsense style of hair and clothing. "I love hearing the piano. It can create such a romantic mood. When the right person is playing, mind you." She gave Jane a shy smile. "I'm a romantic at heart."

"Then I'm sure you'll enjoy staying in this room." Jane opened the door of the Sunrise Room. Its blue and yellow décor was enhanced by the diffused afternoon sun.

Sasha walked into the room and sighed happily. "This is perfect. Such soothing colors." She turned to Jane. "I'm going to like staying here. I'm very pleased."

"Then I'm pleased," Jane said.

Sasha walked to the window and looked out over the

yard. "This town has such a gentle feel. So restful." She turned back to Jane. "I would love to take a walk around town. Do you offer walking tours?"

Jane paused. She did have some errands to run. She supposed she could easily take Sasha along.

"I'm sorry. If it's too much trouble . . ." Sasha looked away. "I don't want to be any trouble."

"Taking you around town would be no trouble at all. We don't offer tours, but if you don't mind doing some boring shopping, you could tag along with me."

"Thank you. As I said, I'm not very adventurous. I always admire people who can just pack up and go places. I'm not like that."

"You're another Beth," Jane said with a smile.

"Pardon me?"

"A bit of an inside joke. I was teasing my older sister Alice that she is like Beth from *Little Women*. She liked being home."

Sasha nodded. "I guess that would be me." Then she spread out her arms. "But look. Here I am. I guess I have a little bit of adventure in me after all. Not enough to go climb Mount Everest, but this is enough adventure for me."

Jane gave her an encouraging smile. "Do you want to rest before we go?"

Sasha laid her suitcase down on the floor and bit her lip. "Should I? The walk won't be very tiring, will it?"

"Not at all. It's just that sometimes our guests arrive here tired and like to rest first."

"I'm not tired. I'm too excited."

If a visit to Acorn Hill made Sasha excited, then Jane could only wonder what her life was like.

"I'll come to get you in about fifteen minutes," Jane said.

"No. I don't want to be a bother. I just want to wash up and do my hair. Tell me where I should meet you."

"I'll be on the front porch when you're ready." Jane went downstairs to get her purse and the shopping cart and wait for Sasha. If taking Sasha on a quick tour of Acorn Hill made her happy, then Jane didn't mind.

As she waited on the front-porch swing, a young couple walked past the inn arm in arm. The sun filtered through the leaves of the trees lining Chapel Road, dappling their figures. They were completely caught up in each other and didn't notice Jane waving at them.

"Isn't that lovely?"

Jane turned to see Sasha standing behind her, watching the couple walk by. She had a wistful look on her face. "I've always dreamed of a love that lasts like that," she said with a melancholy sigh.

Jane got up. "Don't tell me a beautiful woman like you doesn't have a boyfriend?"

"*Beautiful* is not a word people use to describe me, that's for sure. I'm not a very interesting person, that's all." She shrugged. "The things I'm interested in seem tame and boring to others, I'm afraid. I think I'm just going to end up single."

Jane shook her head at Sasha's prognosis for her life. "You seem quite an interesting person to me, and you are not old enough yet to be thinking of spinsterhood."

"I'm in my late twenties."

"You're just a baby yet," Jane said, dismissing her concerns with a wave of her hand. "Are you ready to go?" Jane looked at Sasha's hair, which looked the same as when Jane had left her, perhaps a little neater.

"I'm ready to go."

The weather was as perfect as it could get in Acorn Hill in the spring. The sun was gentle and warm. Birds fluttered past, chirping to one another as they busied themselves with feeding their young.

Jane greeted an older man out for a leisurely stroll, then stopped to talk a moment to Jose Morales, the town handyman. He had just been at Grace Chapel helping Pastor Ley fix one of the lights.

"How long have you lived here?" Sasha asked after they left Jose.

"I was born and raised here, though I did spend a number of years in San Francisco."

"What did you do there?"

"I went to art school and worked in a restaurant as a waitress. I started coming up with ideas for the menu and soon was asked to work with the chef. I learned a lot from him, and when he left I took over his job. I came back to Acorn Hill when my father died. He was the pastor at Grace Chapel. My sisters and I inherited his house and decided to open a bed-and-breakfast."

"I'm sad to hear about your father. Were you close?"

An old sorrow brushed over Jane's heart followed by a deeper happiness. "There was that time when I was away from my sisters and my father. But my father was a loving man, and he kept writing me. I would usually write him back. He kept all the letters I ever wrote him. He was a good example to me of the faithful and abiding love of God."

Sasha was quiet, as if absorbing Jane's words.

Jane laughed lightly. "I don't mean to sound so serious. I had a wonderful relationship with my father. And I'm happy now."

Sasha glanced at Jane's vacant ring finger. "Did you ever want to be married?"

Jane thought of Justin Hinton, the man she had been married to for a short while when she lived in San Francisco. His jealousy of her success as a chef had destroyed their marriage in spite of her best efforts to salvage it. "I was married once," she said, "but the relationship didn't work out." She glanced at Sasha, surprised at what the young woman had pulled out of her. She wasn't usually this open with their guests about personal matters.

"I'm sorry to hear that too." Sasha looked at her. "But in spite of the sadness in your life, you do seem genuinely happy."

"I am. I have a good life and I enjoy what I'm doing. It has its challenges, but overall, yes, I believe God has blessed me richly."

Sasha sighed and tucked her hands in the pockets of her light jacket. "That's good."

Jane halted in front of Fred's Hardware. "I have to make a stop here. I need a light-switch cover for one of the rooms." Jane held the door open for Sasha. "I did tell you that the trip wasn't going to be very fascinating."

"This is fine. I love poking around small towns. I'm not much of a city person, though I do live in one. Everyone has to be somewhere and for me, for now, Harrisburg is where I am." She looked around Fred's store, browsing the crowded shelves full of appliances, bowls, nails, screws and tools. The wooden floor creaked in places. Shelves lined the walls as well, some reaching all the way to the high ceiling. The store smelled of old wood and new plastic.

"What an interesting old building," Sasha said as they walked to the front desk. "Is there anything he doesn't stock?"

"He keeps a wide variety of goods," Jane said, stopping at the end of the electrical aisle. "I need to duck in here. You can go ahead and look around."

Sasha left and Jane quickly found what she needed and a couple of other things besides. Running the inn had expanded her horizons from chef to cleaning-and-maintenance person. A tablet hung by the kitchen phone on which she, Alice or Louise would write things they needed for the house or repairs.

Sasha was admiring the giftware that was artfully displayed on glass shelves when Jane came up front to pay for her purchases. Sasha held up a ceramic teapot, a delighted light in her eyes.

"That's cute," Jane said as she put her purchases on the old wooden counter. The pot looked like a little house, complete with doors, windows and window boxes all molded into the ceramic and painted. The spout was a tree that grew up the side of the house, the handle a vine, and the lid was fashioned out of the chimney.

"I collect them," Sasha said, tracing the painted flowers on the side of the house. "I have the others in this set, but I was missing this one. All the places I looked were sold out." She gave Jane an apologetic glance. "Okay, I know this seems silly, but I love teapots."

Jane rang the bell on the counter. "Then you are going to love one of the other stores we're going to."

"Be with you in a minute," Fred called from the back.

"We can wait," Jane called back. She looked down at Sasha's teapot. "One of the places we'll be stopping is Time for Tea. The owner, Wilhelm Wood, has a variety of tea sets in stock. I hate to steal business from Fred, but you might want to see what Wilhelm has before you buy here."

Sasha pulled out her wallet. "I would, but as I said, I'm missing this one of the set and I can't let it go. Isn't it cute?"

Jane had to agree.

"Sorry to make you wait," Fred said, wiping his hands as he came to the counter. "I was just fixing a mixer and was at a tricky point. Did you find everything that you needed?"

"Yes I did." Jane introduced Sasha as Fred rang up their purchases.

Fred welcomed her to Acorn Hill and indulged in some chitchat while he packed up the teapot in a box. "Vera was telling me that a television producer wants to shoot a reality show here in Acorn Hill. Has this been approved by the town council?"

"For now it is simply a proposal, but I understand that this show is low-key and wouldn't be intrusive."

"Well, the idea does sound interesting. I know Vera was wondering if she would qualify," Fred said with a smile.

"She hardly needs a makeover."

"I'll tell her you said that." Fred handed Jane her change. "That will make her day."

They said good-bye and left the shop.

"People seem to know a lot about each other here," Sasha said as they walked toward the Good Apple Bakery.

"That's one of the difficulties and blessings of a small town," Jane said, setting her bag in the cart. "Do you want to put your teapot in here?"

"No thanks. I'll carry it."

Clarissa Cottrell, the owner of the Good Apple, was sliding another tray of cookies into the display case when they walked in. As usual, her graying hair was worn tied back and knotted under a hair net. She wore a brightly colored apron over a pale-blue house dress.

Though Clarissa was past retirement age, she had no plans for quitting, much to her children's chagrin. She had always said that as long as she could lift the trays out of the ovens, she would keep going.

"This place smells wonderful," Sasha said after Jane introduced them.

"If you're staying at the inn, I'm sure you'll get a whiff or two of some really good smells there too," Clarissa said, pulling on some plastic gloves. "What can I do for you today, Jane?"

"The usual, but you can add a couple of those cookies you've just baked."

Clarissa pulled out two of the cookies. "I'm guessing these are for you and your guest?"

Jane took the cookies directly from Clarissa and handed one to Sasha. "Of course. We need sustenance for our journey."

Sasha bit into hers right away, then closed her eyes in contentment. "These are so good I'm sure they're bad for you."

"When food is baked with love, it has no calories," Clarissa said. "Though I doubt you need to worry about watching what you eat. You're so slender."

"Why, thank you." Sasha looked surprised by the compliment.

Clarissa assembled Jane's order, which also went into the cart. They chatted for a bit. Jane wasn't surprised to find out that Clarissa had already heard, via Ethel, about the possibility of a television show being filmed in Acorn Hill. "I heard it was about makeovers on a budget," Clarissa said.

"Would you be interested?"

"Oh, I think so," Clarissa said, pulling off the plastic gloves and setting them aside. "I could use a few beauty tips. You make sure you let me know when this is going to happen."

"I'm sure Aunt Ethel will keep you posted." Jane said good-bye. Still nibbling on their cookies, they crossed the street, went past Craig Tracy's flower store and down to Wilhelm's shop.

They finished their cookies just as they reached Time for Tea.

"This is the place I was telling you about," Jane said as she opened the door.

The shop's bell tinkled a welcome as they stepped inside. Jane caught the scent of bergamot mixed with a hint of lemon and berry floating above the pervasive, woody scent of fresh tea leaves. Underscoring the elegance of the shop were the faint strains of Vivaldi's *Four Seasons* playing through speakers mounted discreetly throughout the store. Apropos of the season, "Spring" was playing.

Wilhelm was at the counter helping an older woman and gave them an absent smile as she and Sasha entered. He wore a navy-blue blazer with a light-gold shirt and a handsome paisley silk tie. Elegant as always.

"Look at all the tea sets," Sasha said softly, slowly turning around to get a better look. Shelves holding tins of tea from around the world lined the walls, and glass cases held ornate tea sets. Behind Wilhelm were bins of loose tea for those who preferred a custom blend.

Wilhelm's customer thanked him, gave Jane a quick greeting and then left.

"What can I get for you today?" Wilhelm asked, folding his hands on the glass cabinet in front of him.

"Wilhelm, this is Sasha Webber, a guest of ours. She won a stay at the inn in the passport contest that was held last fall. Sasha, this is Wilhelm Wood."

"Congratulations, and welcome to Acorn Hill," Wilhelm said warmly as he offered his hand.

As Sasha shook his hand, Jane could see a trace of pink in her cheeks and an extra sparkle in her eyes. "Hello, Wilhelm," she said in that soft, breathy voice of hers.

Jane set her list on the counter. "Alice wants to try something a little stronger than the blend you made for her last time."

Wilhelm nodded, checked his customer card file for the last blend that he had made, then turned to the bins behind him, humming along to the music as he worked.

"I mark down what I'm doing so that we can repeat or change the blend," Wilhelm explained to Sasha as he mixed the teas.

"Are you planning any exotic trips this year?" Jane asked.

"I had hoped to go to Brazil, but I couldn't get an affordable flight, so I might have to settle for Peru." He weighed the mixture on the brass scale by the tea bins, poured the tea into a small container and sealed it off.

"Wilhelm travels a lot," Jane said to Sasha. "He's been to Europe a number of times, and to Africa a few times as well."

"Kenya, South Africa and Egypt," Wilhelm clarified.

"My, those are some fascinating places," Sasha said, clearly impressed. "Do you have pictures?"

"I have a number of albums that I've put together. And,

I'm afraid, a great number of photos in boxes. I don't seem to have the time to put them together."

"Maybe if you didn't travel so much, you would have time to document your travels," Jane said with a teasing tone to her voice.

"Maybe." He straightened his tie. "How do you like Acorn Hill?" he asked, turning to Sasha.

"It's a lovely town. Such nice old buildings. The town is quaint and peaceful. Just what I like. I'm afraid I'm not the adventurous type." Sasha looked down at her hands.

"Have you done any traveling?" Wilhelm asked.

"I've been to a few other states, but not very many. My father didn't travel much. He says that travel is just pointless moving around and a waste of money." She glanced at him as if perhaps she didn't agree.

"Money spent on travel is money spent on learning. Each place I've been, I've learned so much more than I ever could reading about the countries or watching documentaries on television." Wilhelm gave her a gracious smile, which made Sasha's cheeks even pinker. "I would encourage you to think about traveling."

She lifted her hand to her hair, tucking a wayward strand behind her ear in a self-conscious preening gesture. "I wouldn't know where to start."

"Maybe Wilhelm could give you some hints," Jane suggested.

"Certainly. Most travelers love nothing more than to talk about where they've been," Wilhelm said. "I have kept track of the costs of many of my trips. I could help you decide, depending on what kind of trip you want to make and what your budget is. I've done some backpacking trips on a shoestring and other trips that I've spent more money on."

"That would be wonderful," Sasha said, her eyes brightening.

"Do you still want to buy a tea set?" Jane asked.

Sasha looked down at the various sets in the display case. "There are so many lovely ones here, I don't know if I could make up my mind." She pointed to a blue service. "May I have a look at that one?"

"The Staffordshire?" Wilhelm took the set out and placed it carefully on top of the display case.

"I collect teapots, but I've always wanted to buy a really nice set. I don't know much about china," Sasha said, glancing up at Wilhelm as if to see his reaction.

"Well you have good taste, Sasha. This set is made of bone china, which is of a slightly higher quality than the porcelain set beside it." He held a cup up to the light. "You can see how translucent the china is. Bone china is made up of China clay, which is the purest of the clays. China clay can be easily molded and has a fine texture. The addition of bone ash to the clay gives it added translucency and whiteness over the porcelain clays." He set the cup gently down. "This is an excellent choice."

Sasha touched the delicate cup, tracing its soft mauve iris pattern. "It is so pretty. And I really like the unique shape."

"Yes. The hexagon shape does give the teapot and the cups a distinctive profile." Wilhelm bent down and pulled out another set. This one was brightly colored in shades of gold, green and red. The cups had no saucers, and the pot had a woven bamboo handle. "This one is also eye-catching if you are looking for unique. This comes from Japan."

Sasha touched it as well, frowning in delighted confusion. "I don't know which one I like better." She looked up at Wilhelm. "What would you suggest?"

"I would think cost would be a factor." He quoted her the price of each, and Jane suddenly realized how he could afford his trips abroad. The stock in his store was always changing, and she knew that he also sold his china through the mail.

Sasha looked from one to the other, asking Wilhelm

questions about the differences and how to take care of the sets.

Jane didn't want to rush her, but she did have a few other errands to run. As if sensing her discomfort, Sasha said to Jane, "You can carry on if you want. I'd like to stay here for a while."

"I can wait," Jane said.

"That's okay. I don't want to hold you up." Sasha threw a quick glance Wilhelm's way, blushing prettily as she did. Jane realized what was going on.

It seemed that their newest guest was interested in Wilhelm. Jane had to smile. Wilhelm was good-looking in a distinguished way, and she could see why a romantic such as Sasha would be attracted to him.

"Actually, I do have more errands to run. And I don't want to rush you." She made a show of looking at her watch. "Do you want me to stop by and pick you up when I'm done?"

"I'm sure I can find my way back to the inn," Sasha said.

"Otherwise, I can show her the way," Wilhelm replied.

"That would be very kind." Jane glanced from Sasha to Wilhelm. But Sasha had eyes only for Wilhelm, and Wilhelm didn't seem to mind her attention.

As she walked across the street to the post office, she found herself chuckling. *All the signs point to spring.*

Chapter  Five

Excuse me?"

Alice turned around at the sound of a light, breathy voice. Sasha stood by the swinging door that separated the dining room from the kitchen. She was smiling cheerfully.

"Come in," Alice said, getting up. "What can I do for you?"

"I was just wondering if I could have a glass of ice water." Sasha came into the kitchen.

"Of course you may. There's some iced tea. Would you like some of that instead?"

"That sounds lovely," Sasha said.

"Have a seat," Alice said, "and I'll get some for you. Is Jane back too?"

"I don't think so. We separated in town so that she could go on with her errands while I stopped at Time for Tea."

Alice poured the tea and arranged a plate of lemon squares and raspberry tarts that Jane had made the day before.

"Thank you very much," Sasha said as Alice set the pastries and plates on the table and the tea in front of her.

"And how did you enjoy your tour of Acorn Hill?" Alice asked.

"It is a charming town. And the people are so friendly."

"Did you find what you were looking for in Wilhelm's shop?"

Sasha followed the track of a droplet of condensation on the outside of her glass with one finger, avoiding Alice's gaze. "I found a tea set that was so beautiful, I couldn't resist it. Wilhelm said he would package it for me so I can take it home without worrying about its safety. That was sweet of him, wasn't it? He is such a kind man."

Considering the price of some of the tea sets Wilhelm carried in his shop, Alice wasn't surprised that he took extra care in making sure they survived their journey. But Sasha seemed to think this was courtesy above and beyond his normal dealings.

"Wilhelm is a conscientious businessman."

"He showed me some of his pictures from his travels." Sasha said. "He has been to so many interesting and fascinating places." Sasha took a careful sip of her iced tea. "He said he would be willing to help me plan a trip. I want to go to Paris sometime and don't really know where to start. I think Paris is one of the most romantic places in Europe, and Wilhelm agreed with me."

"He would know. He has been to enough places to be able to make thoughtful comparisons," Alice agreed.

Sasha looked up at Alice and opened her mouth as if she was about to ask her something, then caught herself. Instead, she picked up the brochure from the Beauty Bound party Alice had been to. "Oh, look at all the lovely colors of eye shadow," she said.

Alice glanced at Sasha, surprised that she was interested. Her creamy complexion and full lips didn't look as if they had been enhanced at all. "You don't wear makeup, do you?"

Sasha waved her delicate hand in a dismissive gesture. "No. I don't need to wear it at work, though my friend always tells me that I should. My father has always said that makeup is just vanity and a waste of money."

But in spite of her words, Sasha kept looking at the brochure, her expression almost rapt.

"Where do you work?"

"I work for a carpet-manufacturing company as a receptionist." She chose a lemon square and put it on one of the plates. "It's a good job. I've worked there since I got out of high school. The benefits are excellent, including a wonderful pension plan."

Sasha took a small bite of her square. "*Mmmm.* That's delicious. Anyway, my father always told me to plan for the future," she continued, "so I laid out a plan. Step one was to get a good job. Step two is take a percentage of my wages every month and invest the money. I'm not sure about step three yet. It depends on what happens." She turned to Alice, frowning slightly. "Does that sound like good planning to you?" she asked.

"And what are you saving for?"

Sasha shrugged. "Someday I would like to take a trip, I think. That's why I thought talking to Wilhelm would be so interesting. He knows so much about so many places. Whereas I don't even know where to start."

She flushed prettily, and Alice wondered how a confirmed bachelor like Wilhelm would react to this sweet young woman's attentions.

"Wilhelm certainly has a lot of stories to tell," Alice agreed. "I'm sure he would be a good guide."

"I think so too," Sasha said. She finished off her iced tea and then got up. "I shouldn't take up any more of your time." She eyed the brochure again and Alice offered it to her.

Sasha hesitated for a moment, then, as if making a decision, took it from her. "Thanks. This will be fun to look through."

Alice watched her go up the stairs, convinced that Sasha's life was far more tame than her own.

"Yoo-hoo. Jane, oh Jane."

Jane paused on her way to the public library and looked around. She recognized the voice as her aunt's, but she couldn't locate its source.

"Jane, over here."

Jane glanced across the street. The first thing she saw was an emerald-green turban, then her aunt's smiling face.

Jane waited for a few cars to drive by and then crossed Berry Lane to where Ethel stood with a slim woman who towered over her aunt.

The woman had chin length ash-blond hair, narrow features and deep-green eyes that flitted from Jane to Ethel to the buildings in the town and then back again. She wore fitted jeans and a green leather jacket that skimmed her hips.

"Jane, I want you to meet Noralee Spracht. She's a television producer. The one I was telling you about. She's come from Harrisburg and wants to do a show here. Don't you think that's exciting?"

Jane wasn't so sure she shared her aunt's excitement or enthusiasm. She knew that the filming of a television show would have to be approved by the town council.

"Welcome to Acorn Hill," Jane said, taking Noralee's outstretched hand.

Noralee's gaze flitted over Jane, then Ethel. "Thanks. I'm glad to be here. It's a nice town. I think we could do a great show here."

"Of course, we have to convince Lloyd yet," Ethel said, nodding at Noralee as if to reassure her. "But I'm sure that won't be a problem."

"Talking to the town council will also be necessary," Jane said. "They will have to approve the project."

Ethel frowned as if that was a formality she would rather not deal with.

"I don't have a problem with meeting with them," Noralee said. She paused a moment and held up her hand in a beg-your-pardon motion as she pulled her cellular phone out of the pocket of her coat. She turned away to talk, and Ethel drew Jane aside.

"You're not going to make this hard for her, are you?" she asked, her tone almost pleading.

"Why do you want to do this so badly?" Jane asked.

Ethel glanced over her shoulder at Noralee who was snapping orders into her cell phone, one hand on her hip.

She drew closer to her niece. "Besides hoping that I can get some expert advice on my hair?" Ethel smiled. "It would be good for Acorn Hill and a wonderful opportunity for Betty Dunkle. They want to film the show in her salon. Besides, lots of our friends could be on the show, and I think it would be great fun. Is there anything wrong with that?"

"No, there isn't, Aunt Ethel. If the town thinks the show is a good idea, I have no problem with it, provided it doesn't make our quiet town too busy."

"Noralee said the show would require only a small production crew—a makeup person and some hair people and a couple of cameramen . . ."

"Sorry about that." Noralee flashed them both a smile. "Just a minor glitch back at the studio." She dropped her phone back into her pocket and glanced at Betty Dunkle's shop behind them. "I thought the best venue would be something local. Like this place, the Clip 'n' Curl. It would give the show a hometown flavor."

"How does Betty feel about it?" Jane asked.

"We haven't talked to her yet." Ethel caught Jane by the arm. "Why don't you come with us?"

Jane had no wish to appear to be campaigning for her

aunt. However, Ethel had a firm grip on her arm, and she didn't want to cause a fuss trying to extricate herself.

As they entered the shop, the strains of country music and the pervasive smell of perm solution mingled with hair spray and lavender-scented candles greeted them. Posters of smug-looking young women with clipped and trimmed hair covered three of the walls. The fourth had large mirrors, in front of which were barber chairs. A swag of fake flowers topped each mirror. Pictures of family members of the other hairdresser who worked for Betty were tucked into the frame of her mirror and perched on the shelf in front of her chair. Magazines were stacked into a space below the shelf.

The shop was quiet today. A teenage girl who was getting her hair cut occupied one of the chairs.

Betty Dunkle was bent over the girl, a frown on her face as she evaluated the teen's hair in the large mirror. Her own blond hair was cut short, framing her rounded face. She wore a black nylon tunic and over that an apron that held an assortment of combs and scissors.

Betty was in her late forties and had been working here since she graduated from a hairdressing school. Her father had owned this building, but at that time it was a barber shop. When Betty took over, she made a few changes and, from the look of the older fixtures and the tiled floor, hadn't done much since. The shop exuded an air of worn comfort— from the cracked leather chairs in the waiting area to the glass-block divider wall that had gone from the height of fashion to old-fashioned to retro without Betty having to change a thing.

Betty herself seemed as if she was caught in her own personal time warp. She wore corduroy pants and espadrilles, and Jane was fairly sure that underneath the black smock was a brightly printed polyester shirt that she had picked up at a thrift store somewhere.

Betty had her own personal style and made no apologies for it.

"This cut should be easy to take care of," Betty was saying as she snipped and fluffed and frowned. She pulled two strands of hair down the sides of the girl's face as if comparing lengths, then the scissors flew again. "Just use a round brush and some styling gel." As Betty spoke she glanced over, noticing her guests for the first time. "Be right with you, Ethel. Jane," Betty said as she pulled out a blow-dryer.

As the blow-dryer whirred, Jane glanced around, checking to see if Betty had put up any new posters since she was here last, but the same girls that had been there for the past year still looked down their noses at her.

Jane came to Betty's from time to time to get a trim and some shaping done, but for the most part she didn't spend a lot of time either here or on her own hair.

She glanced at Noralee, wondering at her reaction to this most unglamorous place. To her surprise the woman was smiling as she looked around. Obviously the Clip 'n' Curl met with her approval.

Betty was done in a matter of minutes. The teenager hopped off the chair and stood in front of the mirror, turning her head this way and that as if relishing the new look.

Jane could see from the pile of hair on the floor that only a few moments ago the girl had much longer hair. She felt a moment of weakness as she fingered her own long ponytail, trying to imagine getting her hair cut short.

She couldn't. She wasn't vain, but she did like wearing her hair long. It was easy to take care of, and long hair was, well, her.

The girl shook her head again, then walked with Betty to the front to pay. "Thanks, Betty. I really like the style," she said, slipping the change into her pocket.

"And don't forget, you can come back a couple of times

to get your bangs trimmed for free," Betty said as she shut the drawer of the old-fashioned cash register.

Jane gave the girl a quick smile as she left, the bells on the door jangling as it shut.

"So, Ethel. How's the hair?" Betty said, her eyes going to Ethel's turban.

Ethel grimaced. "I'm not here to talk about my hair. Well, maybe I am here to talk about my hair. Actually, to talk about a bunch of ladies' hair. Ladies from Acorn Hill who maybe aren't so happy with their hair, or possibly maybe even their looks. Though goodness knows, I realize we need to be thankful for what God has given us, like Louise said, but at the same time, I think we can all use a little bit of help. You know all about that, Betty," Ethel said, giving Betty a careful smile. "I mean that's what you do."

Betty crossed her arms over her ample bosom and shifted her weight to one hip as if perfectly content to let Ethel ramble on until she eventually came to the point.

Jane realized that Betty had probably listened to many of Ethel's conversations and was used to how her aunt operated. It took time, but like bumblebees, Ethel's conversations went this way and that and ultimately arrived at their destination.

"But this lady here, Noralee Spracht, she's a producer for a television show. Noralee, this is Betty Dunkle, our local hairdresser." Betty and Noralee shook hands while Ethel rambled on. "Noralee wants to film a reality television show about makeovers, and I suggested that she come to you. Now I know you don't do plastic surgery and things like that, but she doesn't want anything complicated. Just fun kinds of things that could be done in a small-town shop."

Ethel was about to draw another breath and carry on when Noralee, obviously used to a speedier pace, cut in.

"What I'm hoping to do is something a little different from the current crop of makeover television shows. Instead of bombarding the contestants with hairdressers they could probably never afford and makeup they would never buy, I wanted to try a makeover show using the resources available to women in a small town." In one smooth motion, Noralee pulled out a business card and handed it to Betty. "We're not a large television studio and I don't expect that the show will be syndicated, so our resources are limited. That's how I came up with the idea of using a small town. My friend Dominique told me about Acorn Hill, so I thought I would check it out. I would like to use your shop as a base of operations."

Betty glanced at the card and frowned.

"Having the show filmed here could be a lot of fun, Betty," Ethel said, jumping into the conversational breach. "And maybe you could get some new ideas. Not that you don't do a good job, mind you, but it always helps to get other opinions, doesn't it, Jane?"

Oh no you don't, thought Jane, who wisely kept her mouth shut. Getting pulled into the shop was bad enough; she wasn't going to get involved in her aunt's agenda.

Betty looked closely at the card again. "You aren't coming here to poke fun at us, are you? 'Cause I don't want to be a part of the show if that's what you're going to do."

"I understand," Noralee said. "But no. This is going to be done straight up. There will be no laugh track, no unexpected surprises, just ordinary women getting makeovers using ordinary products and services."

Betty tapped the card against her chin as she studied Noralee. "And what do I get out of this?"

"Free publicity, plus the chance to get some new ideas from other stylists. Of course, we'll cover all your operating expenses during the filming, plus we'll compensate you for any appointments that you have to cancel to accommodate us."

"And how much work would I be doing compared to how much your experts would be doing?"

"We would bring in someone to do the makeover cuts, but you would be there to work with her. We would also bring in a makeup consultant and some wardrobe people, but most of the filming would be done here because, after all, a hairstyle is usually the most dramatic change women can make."

Betty looked down at the card again. "Sounds interesting. Sounds different too."

"I think this opportunity could be a perfect thing for you, Betty," Ethel said, unable to keep her comments to herself any longer. "And we would all get some good ideas."

"And you would get something done about that hair of yours," Betty said, grinning at Ethel.

Ethel touched her turban, self-conscious. "Well, perhaps that too."

Betty nodded slowly, as if thinking. "Okay. I guess it could work out. As long as filming doesn't interfere too much with my other customers."

"What I was hoping was that we could get your customers to go along with this as well," Noralee put in.

"I thought you got people to audition for these shows?" Betty asked.

"This isn't quite the same thing as some of the other reality shows. We aren't relying on gimmicks or personalities. The more ordinary the person, the better."

"What do you think, Jane?"

"As long as things don't get too crazy in town because of this, I think it could be fun." Jane gave Betty an encouraging smile. She wasn't about to tell Betty what she should or shouldn't do in her own shop. As for whether the town would agree to the show, well, that was up to the town council. Not her.

"I guess I could give it a whirl," Betty said. "I would like to see a few other businesses in town get involved though."

"Absolutely. We'll be purchasing the cosmetics here in town and the clothes from . . ." Noralee frowned and glanced at Jane. "What is the name of that dress shop? Nellie's?"

"Yes, that's it," said Ethel. "And she has a good variety in her store. Not so desperately modern, mind you, but she does try to carry reasonably stylish clothes."

"Great. We'll talk to her next," Noralee said, glancing at her watch.

"After that, we can set up a meeting with the town council," Ethel said.

Jane winked at Betty. Ethel on a mission was a sight to behold.

Chapter Six

How long has Wilhelm lived here?" Sasha asked, handing Jane her gardening trowel. It was a lovely Friday morning, and Jane had been busy in the garden when Sasha had joined her.

Jane dug out a stubborn weed and threw it toward the pile that was slowly accumulating on the edge of the garden. "He's lived in Acorn Hill all his life."

"And how long is that?"

A not-too-subtle way of asking how old he is.

"Wilhelm is in his forties, I believe," Jane said. She wasn't entirely sure, only that he was younger than she was and quite a bit older than Sasha.

Sasha leaned back on her heels, slowly picking the leaves off a weed. "That's why he's so mature," she said with a sigh. "But in a good way mature, you know?"

Jane glanced sidelong at the young woman, surprised to see a dreamy look on her face.

"Does he have a serious girlfriend?" Sasha asked. "I noticed he doesn't wear a wedding ring."

"I believe he was dating someone a long time ago. I'm not entirely sure if he has since."

"I can't imagine why. He's so handsome."

Jane felt a moment's unease. Sasha was a guest and Jane

did not feel it was her place to give her advice, but at the same time, Wilhelm was a friend. She wondered if he knew what Sasha thought of him.

"I went there again yesterday, and he showed me some of his pictures. Did you know he keeps them in a box?" She shook her head. "I told him I would put them in an album for him. Do you know where I can buy some albums?"

"I believe that you could find some at the General Store; otherwise, try the pharmacy." Jane absently dug out another weed as she wondered whether Wilhelm welcomed Sasha's attention. She chuckled inwardly, thinking of a young woman like Sasha getting starry-eyed over him.

"That's wonderful. I'm looking forward to getting them all organized for him. I know he will appreciate it." Sasha pulled up a weed and slowly turned it over in her hands, a smile curving her lips. "He's so kind to me. Yesterday he told me that I had lovely hair." She gave a light laugh and threw the weed in the general direction of the pile.

"You do," Jane said, again glancing sidelong at Sasha. Out here in the sun, her copper-colored hair shone like fire. "Do you ever wear your hair in another style?"

Sasha fingered her long braid and shrugged. "No. I've always worn it like this."

Jane sat back and studied Sasha a little more closely.

"I think your hair would look absolutely lovely if you wore it loose."

Sasha brightened. "Do you think Wilhelm would notice?"

"Oh, I'm sure he would," Jane said.

"Then I'll have to try it." She got up and brushed the dirt off her pants.

"Right now?" Jane asked.

Sasha frowned. "Should I wait? Do you need me to help you finish with the garden?"

"Of course not," Jane said with a light laugh. "You are our guest. You do whatever you want."

Sasha flashed Jane a smile, spun around and almost ran back to the inn.

⌾

"I'd like to thank you for your hospitality during my stay here," Woody said, handing Louise his room key Friday afternoon.

"Are all the renovations done on your new home?" Louise asked.

"For the most part." Woody took his receipt from Louise and tucked it into the pocket of his jacket. "There are a few things to be done, but the house is habitable now."

"I'm sorry we couldn't let you stay a few more days, but we have more people coming this afternoon."

"I understood that when I came here." He bent over and picked up his briefcase, then hesitated, his gaze resting momentarily on Louise. "Has anyone told you recently that you are an attractive woman?"

Louise felt her neck grow warm both with his scrutiny and his unexpected comment.

"Not for a long time," she said keeping her voice cool. She had no desire to encourage him. She was content with her life the way it was, and the thought of having to rearrange her neatly ordered life around the whims of a man didn't appeal to her.

"Then I'd like to be the first, in a long time, to do so."

Louise held his level gaze. "While I appreciate the senti-ment, I have to say that is the most oblique compliment I've heard in my life."

Woody laughed. "You're right. That was roundabout. Let me try again." He squared his shoulders. "Louise, you are an attractive woman."

"Thank you," Louise said, her eyes not moving one jot.

He waited as if expecting more, but Louise wasn't going to help him out. She didn't want to laugh at his puzzled expression, but she drew the conclusion that he wasn't accustomed to having his advances brushed aside.

"I was wondering if you would be willing to go out with me sometime?"

"On a date?" Louise was surprised.

"That is the accepted format of social interaction between two adults."

"And is that the accepted format for a newspaper editor to ask for a date?" Louise asked, lifting one eyebrow.

Woody looked taken aback. "Editor in the past tense. I'm more persuasive when I write first and then edit. But you haven't answered my question."

"I'm sorry. But no."

Woody waited, a faint frown puckering his forehead. Louise didn't add anything to her reply.

"That's blunt," he said.

"The Bible tells us to 'Let your "Yes" be yes and your "No," no' (James 5:12). I don't need to add to that."

"Why am I not surprised that you're quoting from the Bible?" Woody angled his head toward the front door of the inn. "I noticed your plaque when I checked in. 'A place where God is at home.' Do you really believe that?"

"We do," Louise said, folding her hands on the desk in front of her. "It's our prayer that people who come here be refreshed and encouraged as well."

"Well, I am refreshed. As to encouraged . . ." Woody gave her a quick smile. "You are sure about that date?"

Louise had to give him points for persistence, but in order to underline what she had said, remained silent. If her no was no, to add anything else lessened the impact.

He caught the hint and gave her a look of slightly mocking respect. "You are a stubborn woman, Louise Smith."

"Thank you," was all she said.

"I'll be seeing you again." He gave her a quick salute, then turned and left.

Louise released a sigh as the door shut behind him. She would have to be on her guard with Woody in any future encounters. She had her memories and she had a wonderful life. The last thing she wanted was any romantic entanglements.

Though she had to admit that the feminine part of her was vaguely flattered by his attention.

"Alice. *Psst.* Alice."

Alice looked around and then saw Ethel waving at her from the front door of her house. All Alice could see of her aunt was her head and an arm poking out from the heavy wooden door.

Curious, Alice made her way over the flagstones that made a path between the inn and the carriage house, glancing at the garden as she did. Earlier that day Jane had been working there, but it looked as if she was done now.

"Come in. Come in," Ethel opened the door farther. As Alice came closer, Ethel glanced around once more, her bright eyes flitting over the empty yard, then let her in the house.

"Why all the secrecy?" Alice asked as Ethel ushered her inside.

Ethel closed the door and leaned against it. She hadn't covered her hair today, and Alice tried not to stare at the pink stripes that looked so odd against Ethel's bright-red hair, or at her fuzzy bangs. "I needed to talk to you without Louise around. I noticed she was sitting outside earlier today and I didn't know if she was going to come back out again."

Alice frowned as she sat down on one of Ethel's living-room chairs. She didn't like sneaking around but was willing to humor her aunt until she found out what was going on. "Why don't you want Louise around?"

"Do you want some tea?"

"No, thank you," Alice said. While she usually enjoyed

visiting with her aunt, she had a busy schedule today and didn't have time for a long stay.

Ethel perched on a chair across from Alice. "I wanted to talk to you about that reality television show," she said. "I know that Louise thinks it's silly, and I don't want her to lecture me. You know that usually I'm all for keeping Acorn Hill quiet and peaceful, but I don't think that show would cause much trouble."

"Louise wouldn't lecture you, Aunt Ethel," Alice said.

"Maybe not, but I just don't want to take the chance. I like Noralee and, well..." Ethel's hand crept up to her striped hair as she fidgeted self-consciously.

"And you would like to have something done about your hair."

"Partly," Ethel said. "That was my first reason, but the more I thought about it, the more I realized that it could be a lot of fun. It won't be disruptive, and it could be good for our town. Even Lloyd thinks so."

"But don't you think it would be more peaceful for the town if you just colored your hair again?" Alice asked.

Ethel sighed heavily. "I can't wait weeks for an opening in Potterston. And besides, didn't you have fun at that makeup party? I thought it could be a great idea to do it again. Noralee said that they would do makeup and hair and clothes. Everything."

"The party was enjoyable," Alice conceded.

"So you'll come with me and Noralee to the town council meeting? To help convince them that we should let the show go on?"

She had been neatly cornered, Alice realized. As she held her aunt's pleading eyes, she felt herself wavering.

Ethel sensed her hesitation as well. "You won't have to do any talking," she went on. "I just want you there for moral support."

Alice was touched by her aunt's entreaty. Ethel wasn't

asking for much. All Alice had to do was show up. Reluctantly, she agreed. "But I'm not going to do any talking," she warned her aunt.

"Just come," Ethel said, flashing Alice a comforting smile. "You won't have to say one single word."

"And Alice agrees with me. Don't you, Alice?"

Alice looked around the town council room at the circle of expectant faces. At the table were the regular members of the town council. Behind them were a surprising number of visitors, all interested, it seemed, in the makeover program.

Alice caught a glimpse of Florence Simpson unexpectedly smiling encouragement, of Hope Collins wearing her usual cheerful expression, and of a few other women Ethel had rounded up in her campaign to get the television show approved.

She wasn't sure what Woody Swigart was doing there, but she saw him standing at the back of the room behind the assembled women.

Lloyd Tynan sat at the end of the table, his suit coat open and his vest straining over his barrel chest. His bow tie bobbed as he swallowed, glancing from Ethel to the town council members. They seemed to be of mixed opinion on the matter, judging from their expressions, which ranged from curious to dubious.

"I did speak with the producer of the show," Alice began, "and I understand that a television show like this by its nature is not intrusive."

"Reality shows usually are done in ordinary places and with only a few cameras, right Alice?" Ethel said, bobbing her head once again in Alice's direction.

Alice fought her frustration with her aunt as she tried to find precisely the right words. She took a breath and swallowed, wondering why her mouth felt so dry. She knew all these people well, but being the focus of attention was unnerving.

She cleared her throat and tried again. "That was what I was told, but of course I have no personal knowledge of what goes into filming such a show." She threw a quick glance toward Noralee Spracht, who nodded encouragingly.

On their way to the meeting, Noralee had told Ethel that in situations such as this one, she found that it was best not to make a formal presentation, but to let interested citizens present the case for the show. She said that way townspeople didn't feel they were being assailed by outsiders. She assured them, however, that she would answer any questions that might come up. Ethel wasn't pleased with her tack but wisely sensed that Noralee was not someone she could railroad as easily as Alice.

"How long would filming this program take?" This question came from Clark Barrett, an older man with a thick head of gray hair and friendly hazel eyes framed by bushy eyebrows.

Clark had been helpful to the Howard sisters when they had renovated the inn. Alice knew him to be a solid, easygoing person.

All eyes now turned to Noralee, who glanced at Lloyd as if seeking his permission to speak, which he granted with a quick nod.

"The filming will be sporadic, but it will be finished in a few weeks. I expect we'll come in with two cameramen. The show will be mostly handheld camera work, and most filming will be done in Betty Dunkle's beauty shop, the Clip 'n' Curl. As I told Betty, we'll cover the operating expenses of Betty's beauty shop the entire time the program will be filming. We will also purchase clothing and cosmetics in town, so there's a benefit for the clothing store and the pharmacy. I'm also hoping to do some set pieces with the women involved in some of the local businesses, which would represent free promotion and advertising. For example, a couple of the shops that I really enjoyed and that would make great sets were Nine Lives Bookstore and Acorn Hill Antiques."

Alice saw Joseph Holzmann, a member of the town council, look up from his notes at the mention of his shop. He looked suddenly interested.

The town council members asked a few more questions, and now and again, Alice saw Woody's head lower, as if he was looking at something in his hands.

"And where would the filming take place?" Hank McPheeter asked.

"Here, all over town, but mostly at Betty's," Lloyd said patiently. Hank had been on the town council so long that Lloyd knew Hank was just making sure of his facts.

"I see," Hank said.

After a few more questions from the council and some well-thought-out answers from Noralee, Lloyd drew the meeting to a close. "I would like to thank all of you for coming." His eyes stopped a moment on Ethel, who was looking intently at him. "This was most informative." He gave a puzzled look at Woody, who stood behind Florence Simpson, nearly hidden by her substantial figure. "Before we end the meeting, I'd like to welcome a new member of our community, Mr. Elwood Swigart." There was light applause as people turned toward him as if noticing him for the first time.

"Of course, the council shall have to discuss this among ourselves, but we will let you know as soon as a decision is reached." Lloyd got to his feet, a signal for the people who weren't members of the town council to leave.

Walking out with Ethel and Noralee, Alice waited until they were well past the door of the council chambers, before addressing her aunt. "Aunt Ethel—"

"That went well," Ethel interrupted, giving Alice a huge smile as if she hadn't just put her niece on the spot.

Alice glanced at Noralee, who was also looking pleased, and realized this wasn't the time or place to speak to her aunt.

"Excuse me." Woody Swigart came up to the group, smiling at each of them in a way that made Alice feel he wanted something. "I was wondering, Mrs. Buckley, if you think there is any hope of this show going through."

Ethel looked as taken aback as Alice had been when her aunt put her on the spot only a few moments ago.

And as she had only a few moments ago, she glanced toward Alice, who only shook her head. Not again.

"I think it will," Ethel said primly. "After all, Lloyd knows what I want."

Alice stifled a groan. She knew what Ethel meant, but her comment sounded as if Ethel expected special favors because of her relationship with Lloyd. That was something Woody had alluded to the last time he had spoken with Ethel about the television show.

"I see," was all Woody said, with a faint smirk. He turned to Noralee. "I also understand that there are some women who have a problem with shows of this kind, saying that they are demeaning."

Noralee held his curious gaze but said nothing.

"You don't have a reply for that?" Woody asked, almost in a taunting tone of voice.

"Did you ask me a question to reply to?" Noralee returned, looking as cool as a spring breeze.

Woody's eyes narrowed slightly, his eyes holding Noralee's like a laser, but Noralee neither blinked nor looked away.

He inclined his head as if acknowledging her spunk, then he gave Alice and Ethel a quick glance. "Good morning, ladies," he said, then left.

"I don't think I like that man. But you handled him very well, Noralee," Ethel said, a faint note of awe in her voice.

"Why, you didn't back down one whit, did you? I wonder why he's so curious about this show? Why did he come to a town council meeting when he's barely a resident here?"

"He's settling in Acorn Hill. He's already moved into a house," Alice said. "So maybe he's just interested in the comings and goings of the local people."

"A little too interested," Ethel snapped. "Downright nosy." Ethel turned to Alice and patted her on the shoulder with a motherly gesture. "Thank you so much for coming, my dear," she said. "It was good of you to help out. Now, Noralee, did you want to wait for the council's decision, or did you want to check out the pharmacy while you're here? It has a varied selection of cosmetics, and I'm sure the owner, Chuck Parker, will be more than willing to order in anything you might need."

Without another glance at Alice, Ethel ushered Noralee out of the town hall, leaving Alice bemused and bewildered at how her dear aunt had manipulated her again.

"She's been coming here every day," Wilhelm said, rearranging the display on the counter as he spoke.

"Really," Jane said carefully, trying to get a feel for Wilhelm's reaction to Sasha's interest.

It was Tuesday morning, and Jane was running a few errands. As she was walking down Acorn Avenue, she saw Sasha leaving Wilhelm's store carrying another bag. Jane was certain the young woman had already purchased enough tea to keep her well supplied into the next decade. So, on a whim, Jane ducked into Wilhelm's shop to see how he was dealing with this attention.

"I have to confess, I am flattered. She's a sweet person. But I can't imagine that she's not put off by our age difference," he said.

"She doesn't seem to be." Jane watched him carefully.

Wilhelm nodded slowly. "I am guessing that."

Jane was about to say something else when Wilhelm's gaze flickered to the window.

"What's that?" he asked.

Jane turned and saw a large white van slowly cruise past his shop, then make a turn onto Acorn Avenue.

"That looks like a television van," Wilhelm said.

"Alice mentioned that the town council gave its approval for the television show to be filmed here," Jane said as she walked to the window to see what was going on. "The producer sure didn't waste any time getting started."

Two men exited the van and started unloading power cords and lights.

"I hope this filming isn't too disruptive." Wilhelm frowned as he came to join Jane by the window.

"The producer indicated that it wouldn't be. It looks interesting," Jane said. "I'm going to see what is going on."

"You sound like a tourist."

"The worst kind," Jane happily admitted. "Having a television show filmed here is kind of exciting."

She waved good-bye to Wilhelm, then went on to see what was happening at Betty Dunkle's Clip 'n' Curl.

As she crossed Acorn Avenue, another car pulled up and parked behind the van. Noralee got out and waved to Jane. "Good morning," she called out, pulling a briefcase out of her car. "You're up bright and early."

Obviously nine thirty was earlier to Noralee than it was to Acorn Hill. People had been up and about their business for some time now. Shops had been open for half an hour, and the Coffee Shop had been doing a brisk business since dawn.

"Hi, Noralee. I'm just being a nosy resident," Jane said, watching as the two men brought in another load of sound equipment.

"Come on in," Noralee said.

Jane happily followed her into the shop. Betty Dunkle was busy directing the men, showing them the outlets, the main breaker box and where they could set up.

She gave Jane a quick wave, then ducked into the back.

Jane was fascinated by the process. Noralee conferred with one of the men, consulting a clipboard and gesturing around the shop, pointing out to the cameramen what she wanted where.

"I think this should be an interesting couple of weeks," Betty said as she joined Jane. Betty planted her hands on her hips and looked around her now-crowded shop. "I just hope that my regular customers don't get put off by all the busyness. I know Florence is complaining about the show already.

Jane laughed. "Well, you know Florence. She likes to complain just because she can."

"You're probably right. She did ask some pointed questions about how they are going to choose contestants."

"Did Noralee tell you how that was going to be done?" Jane asked. "Don't reality shows usually hold auditions?"

"She said that it would be quicker just to get the names of the women who are interested, and if we get too many, do a draw tomorrow." Betty pushed a chair aside to make room for one of the men carrying in more equipment. "I put a poster in the window and one up by the register. I've already had a bunch of women tell me that they want to participate, so I've just had them put their names in a box for a drawing."

Betty pointed to a large, loud poster that hung on the wall by the cash register. It said, "*Changing Faces* makeover. Ladies, put your name in for a chance to be a model."

"So who can enter?" Jane asked.

"Anyone, I guess," Betty said.

Jane read the poster again, an idea forming.

You shouldn't, said the grown-up, responsible part of her mind.

Why not? asked the fun-loving part.

She tossed the idea back and forth, and finally the fun-loving part of her won out.

"Where are the entry forms?" Jane asked.

"Do you want to enter?"

"I'm thinking about it," Jane said vaguely.

Betty gave Jane a five-by-seven card, an envelope and a pencil. "You can use the counter to write on. Put your entry in the box when you're done."

Jane hesitated, shrugged and then filled out the card. When she finished, she slipped the card into the envelope and mixed it with the other envelopes in the box before she could change her mind. Calling good-bye to Noralee and Betty, Jane left the shop, pleased with herself and her spontaneous idea. It would be a fun surprise if the name she had entered was chosen.

Her next stop was Craig Tracy's. She had promised to drop off her monthly order for flowers today.

She was still grinning when she entered Wild Things. Craig was leaning back against the counter reading a newspaper. He looked up as she came in.

"Did you see this?" Craig Tracy held up the paper.

"What newspaper is that?" Jane asked as she looked past Craig at the poster-sized calendar hanging behind the counter. "It's only Tuesday. The *Acorn Nutshell* comes out Wednesday."

Craig handed her the paper so she could see its name. "You will notice that this isn't the *Acorn Nutshell*. This is Acorn Hill's newest paper."

Jane frowned as she picked up the tabloid-sized paper with the words *Eye on the Hill* in swooping letters across the top. A double line divided the banner from the headline.

"'Town Council Caves In,'" she read aloud. Her eyes skimmed the article, which was about the town council meeting's deliberations on the proposed reality show. The language of the article was bombastic and inflammatory and referred to "undue influence" and "a council easily swayed by a friend of the mayor."

"Who put this out?" she asked, glancing over the paper once more.

Craig leaned over her shoulder and pointed to the byline written in small letters below the headline.

"By Elwood Swigart?" Jane set the paper down, giving Craig a puzzled look. "Elwood Swigart who was staying at our inn?"

"I don't think there are too many people with that name."

Jane glanced over the rest of the front page. Below the fold, the headline "Toxic Waste Dump" drew her attention. Jane's heart skipped a beat. Was there a proposed waste dump being discussed? She skimmed the article to find that it was a complaint about the irregular garbage collection in town.

Jane opened the paper. Inside, there was a smaller-sized headline, "This Little Piggy." The article questioned the hygiene of a store that would allow a "porcine pet" on the premises. It referred to a recent incident during which Clara Horn's pet potbellied pig, Daisy, slipped her leash and rushed into Viola's bookstore. The article ridiculed "a grown woman pushing a pig around in a buggy." It questioned the competence of a town council that would allow "this ridiculous behavior to occur on a daily basis."

Another feature on the page comprised snippets of news presented one after the other. A few were humorous, but many were full of innuendo.

Jane flipped through the rest of the eight-page paper. A few cartoons and some jokes were used as filler on the next page, preceded by articles dealing with happenings in other nearby towns. Advertisements were sprinkled on the other pages. But the main focus of the paper, and the target of the editor's sarcasm, was Acorn Hill and its residents.

"Where did you get this?" Jane asked, folding the paper and setting it on the counter.

"I bought it at the gas station when I was filling up my car this morning."

"Why?"

"I was curious. The headline sounded interesting. You have to admit, Jane, he does know how to write an article."

"And headlines, obviously," Jane muttered. "I wonder why he's doing this?"

"Apparently he used to be an editor for a paper in Pittsburgh. Maybe he's bored."

"Why doesn't he write a novel like any other self-respecting retired newspaper editor?" Jane couldn't believe the strong language Woody had used. It was as if he was deliberately trying to provoke the people of the town.

"Maybe too tame."

"Or too hard." Jane handed Craig her list. "Here's what we'll be needing for the next few weeks. I am thankful that there are no special celebrations coming up. Perhaps I can splurge on a prickly-pear cactus for our former guest." Jane gave Craig a quick smile just to take the sting out of her comment.

Craig shook his finger at her. "Now Jane, that is not kind."

"You're right, but I really detest that trashy paper."

"Hey, don't put down my taste in reading," Craig murmured as he glanced over Jane's list. "One man's trash is another man's treasure."

Jane groaned. "I'm going to go before you trot out another cliché," she said.

Craig laughed as she left.

As she stepped out of the shop, she almost ran into a knot of people gathered around a person who was reading something out loud. Jane recognized the few snatches that she could hear. Apparently, Woody had sold more than one copy of his rag.

The Coffee Shop was fairly buzzing when she stepped inside. Hope Collins was bent over the front counter, reading a copy of *Eye on the Hill* with avid interest.

Hope looked up as Jane came in and, straightening, quickly slipped the paper under the counter.

"Are you by yourself?" Hope asked, pulling a menu out of the holder by the front counter.

"Sylvia is going to meet me for lunch," Jane said.

"I only have one booth left, so why don't you take it?"

Jane nodded and followed Hope to the empty booth by the window overlooking the street.

At a nearby table, she saw an older couple intently reading something, and beyond them at another table, two women were in deep discussion. From the snippets of conversation that drifted her way, Jane understood that they, too, were talking about Woody's newspaper.

". . . unsanitary you know. He . . . is . . . right," one said, her permed hair bouncing with each enunciated word.

Jane couldn't understand why people would be interested in such negative news coverage, but as she looked around the Coffee Shop, it seemed that every other person was reading Woody's paper.

Sylvia Songer slipped into the booth across from Jane, her eyes bright and her strawberry-blond hair in casual disarray. "You'll never guess what I just read," she said, pushing the ubiquitous paper over to Jane.

Jane didn't even glance down. "I'm guessing an article about 'undue influence' or a 'toxic waste dump.'"

Sylvia looked disappointed. "Oh, you've seen a copy already. I just picked mine up at the Dime Store."

"I saw the paper when I stopped at Craig's shop."

"So? What did you think?"

"I think this is a waste of paper and ink, that's what." Jane flicked her finger at the offending paper.

"I thought some parts were pretty funny." Sylvia twisted her index finger in her hair, studying her friend. "C'mon. I see a twinkle in your eye. I know you were moderately amused by some of the pieces."

Jane shrugged. "Maybe a few parts, but overall, I just don't like the tone. It reminds me of those tabloids that you see by the supermarket checkout with the screaming headlines about a famous movie star punching out a fellow movie star. If you peek inside you find out that the fight was part of the show they were filming. Or they tout some huge medical breakthrough that really is only the speculation of a doctor in an obscure interview."

Sylvia tilted her shoulder in a careless shrug. "Maybe, but I thought the paper was kind of interesting." She looked up at Hope who had suddenly appeared at their table. "Hello, Hope. I'll have a tuna on rye and a coffee."

Jane absently gave her order as well, her attention still held by the paper that lay on the table. She picked up the paper again, reading the story on the back. In spite of her initial reaction, she found herself reading on when she noticed Florence Simpson's name and the comment Woody had made about her.

"You bought the paper too?" Hope asked, brightening when she saw what Jane was holding. "This is the first time I saw it."

"I think this is the paper's first issue," Jane said, setting it back down again and folding her hands as if withstanding temptation.

"Who is the publisher?" Hope asked.

"His name is Elwood Swigart, although he prefers to be called Woody. He was a guest at the inn while the home he just bought was being renovated," Jane told her. "I wonder how he could have gotten all this done so quickly. He's only been here two weeks."

"I wonder if he's going to be printing the paper regularly," Hope said, tucking her pen into the pocket of her apron and moving off toward the kitchen.

"If he is, he'll give Carlene Moss some real competition," Sylvia said.

Jane frowned as the reality of her friend's casual comment registered. "And Carlene's paper comes out tomorrow," Jane said.

"It looks like Elwood Swigart's got most of the important news covered already," Sylvia said, tapping the paper.

Chapter Seven

"What should I do?" Carlene leaned back in her office chair, a copy of Woody's paper on her desk. She ran her fingers through her coarse brown hair, her green eyes atypically dull. "It's Wednesday. My paper comes out today and Elwood Swigart has already covered most of my front-page material."

When Carlene had called the inn that morning, Alice knew immediately why the editor asked Alice to stop by her office. Woody's paper was the talk of the town yesterday. Alice hadn't seen a copy of it, but she heard about *Eye on the Hill* from Jane.

"Not only did he cover most of my news, he mocks the *Acorn Nutshell*." She picked up the new paper and slipped on her reading glasses, their oval frames accenting her heart-shaped face. "This is one of the kinder things he says about my paper: 'The mediocrity of the *Acorn Nutshell*'s articles is equal only to its lackadaisical layout. It is exceeded, however, by the editor's incomplete grasp of the English language.'" Carlene gave Alice a puzzled look over her glasses. "I have never met the man. Why is he so nasty?"

"I have to confess that I'm surprised by his language. It is so extreme," Alice said. During the ten days Woody had stayed at the inn, neither Alice nor her sisters had any hint of the maliciousness he seemed to be showing in his paper.

"'Extreme' is right, but that's his background," Carlene said. "After *Eye* came out, I looked him up. That paper he was connected with in Pittsburgh is a tabloid, not anything a real journalist would be proud of."

"Well, maybe this paper is just a one-time thing."

Carlene pulled off her reading glasses and tapped them on her desk. "His editorial states that he aims to be the 'other voice' he seems to think is needed in Acorn Hill. Does he think we need to hear such harsh criticism of our little town? If he dislikes living here so much, why did he settle here?"

"I wish I could answer your questions," Alice said, feeling inadequate in the face of Carlene's frustration. She knew nothing about newspapers, but she did know enough about business to recognize that a competing paper in a small town like Acorn Hill would cause Carlene problems. "If I may give you some advice," she continued, "it would simply be to carry on. Keep putting out the kind of newspaper you always have. Keep writing about Acorn Hill the way you always have."

"The paper is already out for this week, but I wonder if I shouldn't make some comment about *Eye on the Hill* in my next issue."

Alice pondered that a moment, then shook her head. "I think you might be better off to simply congratulate Woody on the launch of his new paper. Wish him success."

"Even though his success might mean the failure of my paper?" Carlene asked.

Alice felt bad. Giving advice about someone else's business was easy—yet dangerous. However, she knew that Carlene needed her encouragement. "I think if you try to rise above this," Alice said, "you will be the better for it. And the *Acorn Nutshell* will be as well. By choosing integrity, you will not only show him what you are made of, but you will show

Acorn Hill which paper is truly the voice of the town. Because I don't believe his paper is. You were born and raised here. You know the people and their quirks and, what I believe is more important, you love the town." Alice felt the conviction of her words, her voice rising slightly as she brought the point home. "This is your place, Carlene, your town. And that's something Elwood Swigart can't claim. I gather from this first issue that he only sees the negative. Breaking down is always easier than building up. Yes, people will respond to negative comments, but over the long run, people want to be encouraged, helped. Acorn Hill is a good place to live, and I think you are the better person to show us that."

Alice stopped and Carlene stared at her open-mouthed.

They were both silent a moment, as if neither knew what to say to top Alice's comments.

"Well, anyway . . ." Alice fumbled around, embarrassed by her little speech. "That's what I think. For what it's worth."

"Your advice is worth a lot." Carlene sat back in her chair, swinging her reading glasses around by one arm. "And the more I think about it, the more I think you're right. I'll just carry on. It's all I can do. The people of the town will have to decide for themselves which paper they think, as you say, reflects their town."

"I want to let you know I'll be praying that you will find the right words to say," Alice said gently. "I am sure being criticized so publicly isn't easy."

"No. It isn't. I feel, for lack of a better word, exposed." Then Carlene gave Alice a quick smile, dimples flashing from the corners of her mouth. "But thanks again, Alice. You know how I feel about church and all that"—she waved her hand in a vague gesture that acknowledged Alice's offer—"but I appreciate the sentiment."

"Prayer isn't just sentiment or a glib thing to say when there are no other words." Alice didn't want to preach at

Carlene, but at the same time she needed Carlene to know that she hadn't offered this lightly. "It's a genuine communication with the Creator of earth and heaven. That's quite a responsibility, so when I say I'll pray for you, I'm taking on an important task."

"Be careful what you pray for," Carlene said lightly, as if trying to deflect Alice's faith with humor. "You don't want to get bogged down in my sins."

As Alice held Carlene's eye, sympathy for the woman lanced her. Her faith in a loving Father and the peace she had knowing that her sins were forgiven through Jesus were such a part of her she often forgot that not everyone shared that.

"You don't want to either," Alice said with a gentle smile, hoping Carlene understood what she referred to.

Carlene's dimples deepened, and Alice was pleased to see she wasn't offended. "I think I'll take your advice," Carlene said. "I'll carry on as I always have."

Alice got up to leave.

Carlene gave her another smile. "Thanks again, Alice."

"You're welcome."

As Alice left the building, she made good on her promise to pray for Carlene by starting as soon as the door closed behind her.

"Grace Chapel Inn. Louise Smith speaking." Louise tucked the headset of the phone between her chin and shoulder as she carefully ripped a check out of the checkbook. She tucked it with a copy of an invoice into an envelope for mailing. She could hear Jane rumbling around upstairs, shifting the bed in the room directly overhead. Two rooms had been vacated, and tomorrow two new sets of guests would join Sasha and an older couple who had checked in yesterday.

"Louise Smith? You're just the person I must speak with," an unfamiliar voice said. "I want to congratulate you on becoming one of the featured women in our *Changing Faces* makeover program."

Louise was caught midlick. She lowered the envelope and took the handset of the phone firmly in one hand. "Pardon me?"

"You entered the drawing and yours was one of the winning names selected."

"Drawing?"

"The one that was held in Betty Dunkle's hair salon. This is Louise Smith, isn't it?"

"Yes, it is." Louise was about to ask another question when the front door of the inn opened and Viola burst in, a wide smile on her face. Louise could see by her heaving chest that her friend had arrived in a hurry.

"Louise, you're on the show!" Viola announced.

Louise held her hand up, then pointed at the phone. "I'm sorry, what was your name?"

"This is Noralee Spracht," the voice said.

"I'm sorry, I don't know a Noralee Spracht."

"That's the woman who's running the makeover television program," Viola whispered urgently. "I was coming over to congratulate you. Your name was drawn."

Louise frowned, still holding the receiver. "Just a minute, please, Ms. Spracht." She turned to Viola, her hand over the receiver's mouthpiece. "Why are you congratulating me? I know nothing about this program."

"You have to say yes," Viola urged her.

Louise felt disoriented. "Yes to what?"

"The makeover," Viola said, still whispering. With a shake of her head, she took the receiver away from Louise. "May Mrs. Smith call you back in a few minutes?" Viola asked, then jotted down Noralee's cell number on the pad by the phone. "Wonderful, Ms. Spracht. Thank you."

Viola handed the handset back to Louise, who put it down, trying to make sense of what had just happened.

"Viola, could you please tell me what is going on?" Louise asked.

"I was just at Betty Dunkle's to attend the drawing for the makeover program that the television producer is filming."

Louise sighed. "I understand now. I remember Jane, Alice and Ethel talking about this makeover program. A waste of time, I say."

"Well, your name was drawn to be one of the featured women."

"But I didn't enter."

"But you won."

Louise shook her head as if hoping to rearrange her confused thoughts. She and Viola were talking in circles. "I didn't enter the drawing."

"Well if you didn't enter, someone did for you."

Just then Louise heard Jane's tuneless whistle as she came down the stairs.

"Hey, Viola," Jane said, the laundry basket of linen balanced on her hip. "Lovely, lovely day, isn't it?"

"I'm sure days like this make you wish you could be working outside all day," Viola agreed, giving Jane a quick smile.

"I like a balance," Jane said as she paused at the bottom of the stairs, glancing from Viola to her sister. "Louise. You're frowning. Don't tell me I forgot to enter a debit again?"

"No. I think if anything, you were a little overeager in your entering."

"Overeager?" Jane looked puzzled but only for a moment. "Oh. The makeover drawing. How did you know that I entered your name?"

"You could at least have the good grace to look ashamed," Louise said. "I just got a phone call from someone named Noralee Spracht. Viola informs me that she is the producer of the makeover show, and she was calling me to congratulate me on being selected."

Jane almost dropped the laundry basket. "Excellent!" she exclaimed, drawing out the word.

"There's nothing excellent about it," Louise grumbled. "I have no intention of making a fool of myself, trying to curry the judges' favor."

"It's not a beauty pageant," Jane said with a laugh. "There are no judges. All you have to do is allow someone to do your hair and makeup and give you some advice on how to dress."

Louise's frown was not encouraging, but Jane pressed on. "I know you are naturally lovely, Louise, but it's a community event, and it's a chance to embrace your feminine side, get in touch with the inner child who once played with lipstick and makeup." Jane flashed her a teasing expression as she set the laundry basket on the floor.

"I did no such thing," Louise replied.

"That's not what Alice tells me. She distinctly remembers dress-up days with sheets and with scarves pinned to your hair while you two played princess."

"Even more important," Viola put in, "being on the show would be an opportunity to show people that beauty is not the sole right of the young."

Louise's frown faded as she glanced at her friend.

"You are absolutely right," Jane said, sensing Louise's resistance slipping. "You can be the standard bearer of aging gracefully. Show everyone that age is not to be feared but celebrated, that beauty knows no age boundaries, that gray hair is not something to be covered with dye, that wrinkles are an emblem of a full and rich life. Goodness, why am I not hearing a stirring soundtrack?"

"Because you're talking too much?" Louise asked.

"Jane is right, Louise," Viola said. "I think your presence would be an inspiration for older women."

Louise gave her friend a "not you too" look but felt her reluctance wavering.

"Think of it as a celebration of God's gifts," Jane said. "You don't seem to think anything of making your piano students perform in public. How is this different?"

"It's different because we don't choose the face or body we have," Louise said.

"We don't, but we can make the most of what we've been given," Viola said.

Louise looked from her friend to her sister. She wasn't convinced, but she sensed that these two were not going to ease up on her.

"Okay. I'll do it. But only because you two will hound me if I don't."

Jane clapped her hands. "Goody, goody. I get to see my big sister play dress-up." She sobered when she saw Viola's warning look. "Of course, you realize that I use 'dress-up' in the most literal sense," she said, trying to look serious.

"Indeed," Louise said with a lift of an eyebrow.

Chapter Eight

D o you have a moment, Jane?" Wilhelm called out from the doorway of his shop as Jane approached Time for Tea on Thursday.

Curiosity about the makeover show had sent Jane into town for a quick stop at Betty Dunkle's. The nine women whose names had been drawn were gathered there filling out paperwork. Louise had given her a raised eyebrow, making Jane realize that leaving would be a smart thing to do.

Ethel, in spite of her championing the makeover show, hadn't been chosen. Jane had hoped to find her and talk to her about this unforeseen situation, but their aunt was nowhere to be found.

"I have to be back at the inn to make supper," Jane said, taking a quick glance at her wristwatch, "But I can spare a few minutes." It had looked as if Louise would be busy for a while, but Jane wanted to be back at the inn well before Louise arrived.

Wilhelm glanced up the street and then down, then held the door open for Jane.

Once inside, he moved behind the counter, motioning for Jane to follow. Curious about his mysterious manner, she walked around the glass case and into a small office at the back of his store.

The walls of the office were decorated with photos and mementos of his travels. Wilhelm motioned to an antique wooden chair, and when Jane sat down, he did the same across from her. He looked at her, then away as he leaned forward, resting his arms on his legs. He clasped his hands, tapping his thumbs together. Though Wilhelm could be considered excitable, Jane had never seen him this nervous before.

Wilhelm cleared his throat as he adjusted his tie. "I'm afraid this is a delicate situation," he said, glancing around the office once more. He picked up a conch shell that was holding down a variety of papers and turned it over in his hands. "I . . . uh . . . need to talk to you."

"I gathered that," Jane said, trying to put him at ease. If he didn't get to the point soon, she was going to be late making supper. "What did you want to talk to me about?"

Wilhelm put the shell down and sat back in his chair. "It's Sasha."

Jane waited for him to elaborate.

He didn't.

"What about Sasha? I know she has been spending a lot of time here," she prompted.

Wilhelm jumped to his feet and ran his hand over his hair while pacing the office. "That's exactly what I need to talk to you about. She is a lovely woman, and I enjoy her company. But I just . . ." He turned to Jane, his expression pained. "I don't know if I'm being vain or reading too much into the situation, but I think she feels more for me than I feel for her."

Jane felt a moment of acute disappointment for Sasha, who was so clearly enamored of Wilhelm.

"While I'm flattered that she finds my business and my company and my stories interesting, I simply don't think that a woman of her age should be spending so much time with a man my age." Once Wilhelm got started, the words seemed to spill out of their own accord as he walked back and forth in the small space. "I gave her other ideas for entertainment, but she said that she liked coming here. So I can only assume that it's not the history of tea or the care of fine china that holds her fancy. I've caught her looking at me a number of times in a way that I can only construe as romantic."

Jane nodded sadly. "I think you're right."

Wilhelm dropped back in his chair and, leaning back, clasped his hands behind his head. "So what should I do?"

"I take it you're not interested."

"No. I've had my chance at love . . ."

"And . . ." Jane rotated her hand, encouraging further disclosure.

Wilhelm gave her a sad smile. "It's not romantic, I'm afraid. In fact, my story borders on the cliché."

"Do you mind telling me about it?" Though Jane had been away from Acorn Hill for a few years, she thought she knew most of the residents' histories. Wilhelm's romance was something new to her.

"Not many people in Acorn Hill know about this," Wilhelm said, looking beyond Jane as if looking into the past. "I had the usual high school dates but never formed any deep attachment. Then I went to college and met a girl named Arda. She was an exchange student from the Netherlands. It was, for lack of a better phrase, love at first sight. We spent all our available time together. She was intelligent, articulate and beautiful." Wilhelm gave Jane a shy smile. "She told me that she had never loved anyone like she loved me. After six months, I proposed and she accepted. My parents came to college to meet her and paid for a trip to the Netherlands so I could ask her parents for their blessing on our marriage. When we came back, I made plans for our future, and she made plans for our wedding. Everything was in place. Then, about a week before the wedding, she told me that she couldn't marry me. She had met someone else and was deeply in love with him." Wilhelm sighed. "It shook me to the core. I had thought that what she felt for me was unique, that what we had was special. It took me a long time to get over the hurt. By the time I did, I realized I didn't want to put myself through that again. Then, the last time I went to the Netherlands, I met her again. She's still lovely and she's now single." Wilhelm stopped and for a moment all was silent in the shop.

"And you still love her?" Jane asked quietly.

"I think I do," he said. "I don't think much is going to come of my feelings. She loves her life in the Netherlands and I love my life here. I started writing her and she has been answering. I think I'm too set in my ways to change, but for now what we have is a comfortable relationship."

"And Sasha doesn't fit into this picture."

"Not at all," Wilhelm said with a rueful shake of his head. "Though I have to confess I am puzzled by her attention."

"It's not so puzzling. At the risk of sounding like I might have designs on you myself, you're an attractive man," Jane said, her wink adding a bit of levity to her compliment.

"Why thank you, Jane. I'm not above feeling flattered by that comment, coming from you." His smile showed her that he took her compliment the right way. "Though I'm still surprised at her attention."

"I think the fact that you travel adds to a certain mystique that appeals to her as well. You're knowledgeable in your field. I think you strike a romantic figure for a young woman who works at a job she doesn't seem to enjoy."

"I'm sorry to hear that. It makes it doubly hard to tell her that I'm simply not interested in pursuing a relationship with her, other than as a mentor or friend."

"So how do we let her know?" Jane folded her arms over her chest, frowning. "She genuinely likes you."

"If I may be an armchair psychologist, I think the girl has low self-esteem. I made the mistake of telling her that she was beautiful, which she is, I might add, and I think that started this so-called infatuation."

"Any woman would love to hear that, but she probably did read too much into the compliment," Jane agreed. "I'm not sure how you should approach telling her. I'll think about the problem, and maybe I can come up with an idea for you."

"Thanks, Jane," Wilhelm said, standing up at the same time Jane did. "I want to deal with this in a sensitive manner. If by some chance . . . uh . . . you find the right opportunity to tell her. . . well, I'd appreciate it. It might be easier coming from you."

"Somehow, Wilhelm, I don't think such an opportunity will arise." Jane gave him a smile, then went out the door. All the way to Grace Chapel she thought of Sasha.

"My being on this show will require a great deal of time," Louise said, frowning at Jane.

Jane appeared to be absorbed in checking the apple pie on her plate. "Does this pie crust seem a little less flaky than usual? I used a different brand of shortening."

"The pie is just fine. The lamb shish kebab and the couscous were excellent."

As usual, Jane had made a marvelous dinner with that extra bit of seasoning and artistic presentation that lifted the meal from tasty to magnificent.

"So now that we have the menu out of the way, I want to let you know that, because of this program, I will have to cut back on some of my duties at the inn," Louise said.

Jane looked up from her pie, glancing from Alice to Louise. "We knew that," she said.

"Which means you'll have to do even more work," Louise continued.

"That's okay," Alice said with a casual shrug. "Jane and I can manage."

"But you have your work at the hospital, and Jane, I know you were talking about getting more painting done,"

Louise said. "Besides, I think Aunt Ethel should have been chosen. She was so in favor of the show, after all."

"There's nothing we can do about that," Jane said. "The drawing was Noralee's idea, and she's the producer. I guess that was a chance Aunt Ethel took."

Louise was quiet a moment, then took a breath. "A cameraman is going to be spending a day with me tomorrow, filming me as I go about my regular routine—as regular and routine as it can be being followed by a man with a huge camera. So does that change anything?"

"Nothing."

"Did I tell you how large those cameras are?"

Jane held her gaze, one corner of her mouth twitching. "This isn't going to work, Louie. You're not going to get out of this show."

"But it seems like such a waste of time. So much emphasis on hair, makeup, clothing. Surely women are more than that?"

"What bothers you more?" Jane asked. "The fussing or the fact that deep down you kind of like the fussing?"

"I do not like all that fussing," Louise fumed. "If someone in this house had not put my name into that drawing without my permission, I wouldn't have to put up with all of this fuss and bother."

Jane nodded slowly. "The lady doth protest too much, methinks."

"Methinks the same," Alice agreed, laughing at Jane.

Jane turned back to Louise. "Admit it, sister, you're looking forward to facials, eyebrow plucking and leg waxing."

Louise pulled back. "Leg waxing? What in the world does that entail?"

"Legs and, *uh*, wax, I believe." Jane put her hand on Louise's shoulder. "It will be fine. Perfectly harmless."

The look on Louise's face indicated that she wasn't convinced.

"It will be fine," Jane repeated

"That's easy for you to say, Jane."

"Oh, by the way, has either of you seen Sasha?" Jane asked, trying to change the subject. "There was a phone message for her from her father. He wanted her to call him."

"The last I saw her she was heading for Wilhelm's," Alice said.

Louise couldn't stop a faint frown. "I'm surprised Sasha is so forward with Wilhelm. She seems so reserved in other areas."

"I wonder what Wilhelm thinks of the attention," Alice said.

"He doesn't like it," Jane told them.

Louise looked with faint surprise at her sister. "How do you know?"

Jane stood up and walked to the swinging door separating the kitchen from the dining room, did a quick check there, looked into the hall and then went back to the table. She leaned forward and lowered her voice. "While you were at Betty's, Louise, I stopped in on Wilhelm. It seems that at one time he had a true love affair that ended unhappily for him. He's since reconnected with the woman, and while he says they will probably not carry on where they left off, he told me that he has no desire to start up with anyone else, especially someone as young as Sasha."

"She is quite a bit younger than he is," Alice agreed.

Louise shook her head. "Has he told Sasha this?"

Jane shook her head. "He doesn't want to hurt her feelings, but he also knows that he has to tell her sooner or later. He just doesn't know how to break the news to her."

"Maybe he will tonight."

"Maybe, but I doubt it," Jane said. "Wilhelm is such a soft-hearted man, I'm not sure he has the will to tell her."

"Surely he doesn't expect you to do the deed?" Louise asked with surprise.

"Well, he gave me permission to tell her if the right opportunity came up, but he was really asking me for advice on how to break it to Sasha himself."

The front door opened, and each of the sisters glanced in that direction.

Light footsteps tripped across the hardwood flooring of the front entrance, then headed down the hall. Seconds later, Sasha knocked on the open kitchen door. Her bright smile told Louise that Wilhelm had not given her the news.

"Good evening. I was just going to go up to my room, but I was wondering if I could have some ice water?"

"Certainly." Alice was the closest to the refrigerator so she got up and got a pitcher of chilled water from it.

"Would you care to join us?" Jane asked.

Sasha's smile grew even wider. "I would love to," she said, stepping inside the kitchen.

She wore a shapeless brown sweater with a pair of outdated pleated khaki pants that tapered at the ankles. While Louise wasn't up on the latest fashions, she did know one thing about Sasha's clothes: They didn't flatter her at all.

"Would you like some pie?" Jane got up and pulled a chair to the table for Sasha.

"I'd love a piece. I skipped dessert at dinner, and it smells so good."

"And in what nefarious activities have you been indulging?" Jane asked as she served up a fat wedge of pie onto a china plate. She shook a can of whipping cream and with deft movements added a swirl of cream to the top of the golden crust.

"None," said Sasha, looking shocked. "I just was at Wilhelm's. Then I went to the Coffee Shop for some supper."

"Jane is just teasing you," Louise said. "She likes to do that."

"Of course." Sasha emitted a nervous laugh. "I take everything at face value, and I often don't pick up on that kind of thing. I guess I am a bit slow."

Louise frowned. "Don't talk that way," she said. "You're a bright young woman."

"Thanks for that, Mrs. Smith." She took the pie from Jane and thanked her.

"How was your afternoon?" Jane asked.

"Fine. As I said, I stopped at Wilhelm's. I needed to ask him something about the china set I bought the other day." She lowered her fork and shook her head. "I'll tell you, if I had known fine china was so much work to care for, I might have changed my mind about buying it. Wilhelm recommended that when I wash the china I use a mild detergent and line the sink with a towel."

"Yes, it does take extra care," Louise agreed. She sensed that the care and cleaning of fine china was not the cause of the frown marring Sasha's usually smooth forehead.

"I was thinking of buying another set," Sasha continued, "but I think I'll wait to see how things work out with this one." She looked up at the sisters, her smile back in place. "Besides, that would give me another excuse to come back to Acorn Hill. Wilhelm said he would be glad to help me get a set of china started. He knows so much about so many things, so much more than I do."

Louise glanced at Jane, who was looking at Alice, who was looking at Sasha, a touch of sympathy in her eyes.

"He should know a lot," said Jane. "He's had many, many, many years to travel and gain knowledge and experience and a vast array of souvenirs."

In spite of all those *manys*, Sasha didn't seem to get the hint.

"I know," she said brightly. "He has so many neat things in his house."

"Yes . . . he . . . does . . . You saw his house?" Jane asked, the look on her face telling Louise that this was a rare occurrence.

"When I was in his shop, his mother was there as well, and she invited me to come and visit, so I said I would."

"How did he feel about that?" Louise asked.

Sasha toyed with her pie. "I sensed he was a bit uncomfortable. He was clearing his throat a lot and fiddling with his necktie. Kind of nervous behavior I thought."

No one seemed to know what to say, so they said nothing. Sasha took another bite of her pie, then put the fork down. "This is really delicious, Jane, but I'm sorry. I guess I had too much dinner." She blinked, then looked down, but not before a tear left a track on her cheek.

Louise took a chance and gently laid her hand on Sasha's arm. "Is something wrong, my dear?" she asked quietly.

Sasha only sniffed.

Louise reached into the pocket of her sweater, pulled out a clean hanky and handed it to the young woman.

The silence in the room was broken only by Sasha's faint sniffling.

"I'm sorry," she said finally, swiping at the corners of her eye with the hanky. "I shouldn't be such a baby. It's just that . . ." she stopped again, her voice hitching.

"You enjoyed Wilhelm's company, and it seemed that he enjoyed yours," Jane said.

Sasha nodded, bunching the hanky in her hands. "He was so reserved. I knew I made a huge mistake accepting the invitation. He must think I'm very aggressive."

"I don't think Wilhelm thinks less of you because of your visit," Jane said.

Sasha's look of hope was heartbreaking.

Jane took a slow breath, as if for courage, and plowed on. "I think what may be making Wilhelm uncomfortable is that he . . . that he . . . that he is much older than you and that he has had, well . . . he likes to travel."

Louise thought that her sister was about to tell Sasha about Wilhelm's first love, but then Jane continued. "He enjoys freedom and . . . well . . . travel . . ."

Sasha's frown revealed that Jane's explanation didn't satisfy her.

Jane looked at Louise, who, realizing that the truth was the only explanation that would do, nodded at her sister.

Jane drew in a long, slow, breath, and then said quickly, "Even more important, Wilhelm still has strong feelings for a woman he almost married when he was younger."

Sasha's brown eyes welled up with tears again.

"He is still in love? With someone else?" She swiped at her eyes and sniffed again. "He never said anything about that to me."

They said nothing. It was clear to the sisters that Sasha needed some time to absorb this unwelcome news.

"He was always so attentive. I really felt like I was special."

"Wilhelm is, by nature, a kind and considerate man," Louise said. "I am sure that he was sincere in his attentions to you. I'm sorry that you read more into his actions than he intended."

Sasha looked down at her pie, her expression forlorn. "I knew it was too good to be true," she said quietly. "I should have known he wouldn't be attracted to me. I mean, why would he? No one else ever has been."

"Why do you say that, Sasha?" Alice asked. "You are so pretty. I'm sure there are many young men interested in you."

"If they are, they never let me know." Sasha drew in a quivering breath, and before anyone could say another word, she pushed herself back from the table and ran up the stairs to her room, leaving behind three very concerned sisters.

Chapter Nine

Late Friday morning, Louise closed her eyes, counted to ten and then turned to Elton, the young cameraman dominating the parlor with his large body and unwieldy camera. She made herself smile, realizing that even this reprimand would go on tape for someone else to see. She was starting to feel sympathy for celebrities who lived their lives with people watching them all the time. The constant scrutiny was unnerving, but what was even harder was the lack of spontaneity the scrutiny created.

Earlier, she spent time with Elton, Noralee and the ever-present camera, answering questions about her life in Acorn Hill and how she had come to stay here. It was tiring but at the same time, curiously satisfying.

"I can understand that you want to get a slice of my everyday life, Elton," she now said primly, "but you are intimidating my student."

Karly Andrews, age five, sat wide-eyed at the piano, staring at the camera. For the past fifteen minutes, Karly had been more interested in watching Elton De Jonge wield the large piece of equipment than she had been in her lesson.

"Sorry, ma'am," the young man said with an apologetic smile, "But I have to get enough footage for the producer to edit."

"Surely you have enough by now?" Louise didn't want to sound short-tempered, but after having the young man follow her around while she ate breakfast, did chores at the inn and now taught her piano student, she'd had enough of someone watching over her.

"I do, but this little darlin' is so cute, I'd really like to get more of the two of you together. Her mom was happy to give permission for the filming."

The cameraman's faint drawl was charming. Against her will, Louise felt herself weakening.

"It's a real great shot, Miz Smith," he said. "Lemme work it as much as I can."

Louise meant to give him an annoyed look, but when she turned to him, he had his face angled around the camera and his deep-blue eyes, bright smile and dimples softened her. "Please?" he said, his smile growing even wider.

Louise sighed. This young man had disarmed her with his southern charm and easy manners.

"Okay, but I am going to ask that the television show reimburse this young lady's lesson, as today has been unproductive," Louise said, trying to sound forceful.

"Depends on your point of view," Elton said, tugging his backward baseball cap tighter over his head. "It's been productive for me. I've got some great footage. You're a natural for the camera, Miz Smith. Real pretty. Can't wait to see what you look like once those makeup and hair people get hold of you."

Goodness sakes, was this young man making her blush? From the faint heat warming her cheeks, it seemed so.

"Well, that's all well and good, but I have a lesson to teach," she said turning back to Karly, who was waggling her fingers at Elton.

Twenty minutes later the lesson was over. To Louise's relief, they managed to make some progress. Karly slowly came to ignore the large black camera panning in on them from various angles and managed to concentrate on her piano piece.

Louise didn't have the same success. She was ever mindful of the large black eye watching her.

But even with the lesson finished, she wasn't free of the beast. When she slipped her jacket on, Elton was watching her. When she stepped out the door, Elton was there.

She walked down the steps and went around the house. There, she paused a moment, letting the warmth of the sun wash over her.

Dear Lord, give me strength for this. She prayed as she ignored Elton, preferring to focus her attention on the rich smell of the newly turned dirt of the flower beds, the warm touch of the sunshine, the muted squeals of two children playing that bounced through the morning.

It was April. Spring. A season of hope and expectation. It seemed that all creation was celebrating the new life that was promised at Easter last month. She tucked her hands into the pocket of her light jacket and let an unformed prayer of thanks drift upward.

God's creation was good, and she was thankful to be a part of it.

"Uh, Miz Smith. You okay?"

Louise glanced back to see Elton peer around his camera and look at her again, his frown clearly showing his puzzlement.

"I'm fine. I was just praying a moment."

Elton nodded. "Cool," was all he said. "By the way . . ." his sentence drifted off, and Louise wondered why. She caught him looking beyond her and followed the direction of his gaze.

Sasha was walking down the sidewalk, head bowed, her hands in the pockets of her pants. Louise looked back in time to see Elton turn his head to follow her progress. He caught Louise looking at him. A faint flush stained his cheeks before he cleared his throat and turned the camera on again.

She had to smile as she walked to Betty's. She was aware of Elton behind her, stalking her. Elton didn't seem hampered by the camera and easily kept up with her brisk pace. She ignored the curious glances from various residents of Acorn Hill who didn't seem to know what was happening.

When she arrived at the shop, Noralee was talking on her cell phone while Betty sat in her styling chair, swiveling back and forth. As they came in she looked up and smiled at Louise. "Ready for your big day?" she asked.

"I suppose I have to be. Where are the others?"

"We thought it could get too crowded, so Noralee decided to do only one at a time." Betty rose from the chair. "Which works out better because I'll have space to do my other customers."

Noralee snapped her cell phone shut and then smiled at Louise. "Ah. You came," she said in a tone of voice that gave Louise the impression that Noralee was surprised.

"Of course. Once I commit to something, I stick with it."

"I'm glad. Elton, you can set up over here." Noralee glanced back over her shoulder. "Kim. Could you come here please?"

A door opened from the back of Betty's shop and a woman dressed in black, who looked about thirty-five years old, strode into the room. She had black hair—with a wide stripe of electric blue down the center.

Louise drew back at the sight. The hair was bad enough, but as Kim came closer, Louise could see the young woman had five earrings in each ear. Her eyes were heavily ringed with black and her lips were deep purple.

"Louise, this is Kim, our makeup girl. She'll be showing you how to apply products and how to choose colors." Noralee turned to Louise and must have seen her surprise. "I know she's a bit of a shock, but she's an excellent makeup artist. She's worked for a number of television shows, and we're lucky to have her."

Kim reached out and shook Louise's hand. "Howzitgoin?"

Louise paused a moment, then realized that what she thought was one word was, in fact, four. "It's going well," she said with a nervous smile.

What in the world had she agreed to? There was no way she was going to entrust her face to this girl who had such blatant disrespect for her own.

Kim snapped her gum as she put on what looked like a carpenter's apron. But instead of holding tools, it held makeup brushes—about thirty of them in assorted sizes and shapes.

Behind her was a table with an assortment of cosmetics spread out over it. These, as promised by the television producer, had been purchased locally.

"So we'll start with hair?" Kim said, shifting her weight from one foot to the other. "What do I do in the meantime?"

"Look pretty, Kim," joked Elton. "It's what you do best."

Kim gave him a bored look but didn't deign to reply.

"So where's Angela? Isn't she supposed to be doin' hair with Betty here?" Kim asked, snaps from her gum punctuating her comments.

"She'll be coming," Noralee said, but she glanced at the door as if doubting her own optimistic comment. She turned back to Kim.

"While we're waiting for Angela, you can do some prelim work with Mrs. Smith."

Kim snapped her gum and lifted her chin toward Louise. "You may as well come here, ma'am," she said.

Louise glanced from Noralee to Elton who nodded encouragement at her.

"Don't worry 'bout Kim," Elton said. "Her bark used to be as bad as her bite, but she's been muzzled so you're okay."

"You're such a loser, Elton," Kim groused as she turned the chair around for Louise to sit down. "When you gonna get yourself a real job?"

Elton just laughed and hoisted his camera onto a stand. "When you get yourself a real hair color."

Louise sat down in the chair, but Kim remained motionless. Louise glanced around, wondering what was going on.

"I'm waiting for wonder boy here to get set up," Kim explained, jerking a thumb over her shoulder at Elton, who was rolling the camera over the floor. "We've got to film all of this."

She threw a bored glance over her shoulder, then heaved a heavy sigh. "You ready, Elt-man?"

"Ready, Super Kim."

Bright lights flashed on, almost blinding Louise. She blinked, then tried to find the source of the sudden light.

"He's just getting you lit up properly so that we don't have too many shadows," Kim explained, turning Louise's chair around to face that large black eye once again.

And again they waited.

After about ten minutes, Noralee joined them. Another woman stood at her side. "Louise, this is Angela. She is going to be doing your hair."

Angela was as nondescript as Kim was colorful. Her beige shirt and skirt did nothing for her sallow skin tone, and her hair was pulled back in a severe ponytail. If this was the woman who was to transform her, then Angela inspired even less confidence than Kim had.

"So. This is the lady?" Angela looked Louise over, then frowned. Without any warning, she reached over and lifted Louise's hair, ran her fingers through it, and tilted Louise's head this way and that.

Louise had to fight the urge to jerk her head away.

"I don't know, Nora. This is going to be hard. I don't know why you picked me to do this. You know I don't like working outside of my own salon. I wish we could have done the show there. I have all my own things there." Angela's mouth turned down at the corners, expressing her distaste more eloquently than her words.

Noralee gave Louise a conspiratorial wink, then put her arm around Angela, giving her a quick hug. "I picked you because you're the best I know. You can do wonders with even the most difficult hair. You can do magic."

Angela's petulant expression didn't thaw under Noralee's effusive praise. Instead she heaved a sigh that indicated how put upon she felt. "Okay. But don't blame me when the cut turns out lousy. This is just not a good place to work."

Louise glanced from Noralee to Angela, but Noralee didn't seem disturbed by Angela's peevishness. Louise was glad that Betty was busy across the room and out of earshot.

"You'll be just great," Noralee said, patting Angela on the shoulder. She looked from Kim to Angela to Louise. "What we're going to be doing is filming the highlights of each makeover," she explained. "We'll be doing one a day until we're done. That way it's less work for Betty and we don't tie the shop up for so long. Mornings will be spent on makeovers. Afternoons will be spent on interviews with the next contestant. We'll be able to keep a good flow that way."

"And what do we do in the meantime?" Angela asked. "You're going to be running around, talking to people while we sit here and twiddle our thumbs? The hotel I stayed at last night didn't even have cable for goodness' sakes. I ended up eating most of the stuff in the snack bar, and you know how I have to watch my weight."

"It's just for a while, Angela. And you're getting paid to do this."

"Not enough, I think."

Louise felt a new admiration for Noralee, putting up with such a variety of disagreeable people. Her cheerful expression never faltered.

"I want to move out of there," Angela continued. "But there's no other place to stay nearby. Kim doesn't like driving back and forth from Pottstown either."

"I believe it's called Potterston," Noralee said. She

turned to Louise. "You told me that you and your sisters run a bed-and-breakfast. Do you have room for a few people, and would you be willing to do dinner as well?"

"We do have two empty rooms for the next few days," Louise said, "due to a last-minute cancellation by a party of three. I'll check my schedule to see how long the rooms will be empty. My sister does the cooking, so I'll have to ask her about serving dinner. We would have to charge more, you understand, if we include the extra meal."

"Do you have cable?" Angela asked.

"No."

Angela's expression told Louise precisely what the woman thought of that situation.

"The inn would be a lot closer for you and Kim," Noralee offered helpfully.

"How far?" Kim asked.

"We're just down the road," Louise said. "You can walk here."

"Walk?" Kim asked, sounding incredulous.

"Walking is that thing you do when you want to get from your car to the mall," Elton called out from behind his camera.

Kim gave him an exasperated eye roll.

"I leave the decision up to you two," Noralee said to Kim and Angela. "I don't mind driving from Potterston. I need Internet access in my hotel room, so moving is not an option for me. When we're done with Louise, you two can go to the inn and see for yourself. I've heard that it's a beautiful place."

Kim's halfhearted shrug told Louise nothing. And Angela's bored expression told her even less.

"Time's movin' on," Elton called out. "We need to get this wrapped so I can get Hope in the restaurant while she's still working."

Suddenly Noralee was all business. She snapped out quick orders. Angela took her place beside Louise and called Betty to join them.

The camera started filming and Angela started talking. "What I think we should do in this case is work with her natural coloring. Because Louise is an older woman, we don't want to work against her skin type or create too many changes." Angela again lifted Louise's hair but this time was less abrupt. "Louise is fortunate to have thick hair, which is unusual for a woman of her age. Thinning is a challenge for hairdressers of more mature women."

Angela and Betty chatted together, discussing what would be the best course of action.

Louise felt like a science-fair project but for the most part was interested in what Angela had to say. Then they spoke of hair color and skin tones and washes and rinses, and Louise grew bored. But, ever aware of Elton filming, she pasted what she hoped was an interested expression on her face and held it.

"Now, the next step is to determine the best way to work with your regular routine." Angela turned back to Louise and asked her about her beauty regimen.

"I wash my face in the morning . . ."

"With soap and water?" Kim interrupted.

"Yes."

"Bad move," Kim said. "At your age, soap leaches all your natural oils out of your skin."

"At my age, leaching oils can't be good," Louise said in an attempt at humor.

Kim's smile told her that she had halfway succeeded. "No, it can't."

"How much time do you spend on hair and makeup?" Angela asked.

Louise thought. "Not much."

"That doesn't help me. Describe your typical morning as far as hair and makeup are concerned."

Louise had to think. Her mornings were so automatic she never considered how much or little time she spent on herself. "I wash my face in the shower. Comb my hair. Sometimes put on some lipstick. On special occasions I put on mascara."

They asked her how much time she had and how much time she could spare. They asked about her clothing, about her preferences for color, about her hobbies and how she spent her day.

Angela fiddled with her hair some more and then, when it seemed they had gotten every last bit of information from Louise except her Social Security number, they got to work.

Angela was first up.

The first thing Angela instructed Betty to do was a scalp massage. While Betty was massaging, Angela pointed out Louise's features.

"You'll notice that Louise has a strong chin and defined cheekbones. This has allowed her to age gracefully but at the same time maintain a face that radiates authority."

Louise wasn't sure she liked the fact that her face radiated authority. She preferred it radiated something else, but there it was. Angela had spoken.

Angela and Betty chatted, and slowly Louise began to understand why Noralee had put so much faith in this dour woman. In spite of her put-upon attitude, she spoke knowledgeably and with confidence.

After the scalp massage, Betty washed her hair—again under the guidance of Angela and again with Elton watching through his camera. Louise wanted to express her reservations about having the young man filming her emerge from her final rinse looking like a drowned terrier. Except she didn't know what was worse: the potential of having thousands of viewers see her wet head, or for them to hear her voice her insecurity at having her wet head filmed.

She opted for another fake smile and chose, from then on, to try to ignore the camera completely.

Betty and Angela discussed coloring Louise's hair but

agreed that Louise's silver hair was stunning and that they would only be cutting today.

Betty started snipping and cutting. Every now and then, Angela would demonstrate another technique. Louise found herself interested in spite of herself at the mechanics of the haircutting.

"If we give her a few more layers"—Angela took a pair of scissors from her own apron and started snipping and cutting in what seemed a most cavalier fashion—"her hair will fall more gracefully. And given that Louise doesn't fuss with her hair, this will, in effect, give everyone the idea that she does." Angela tucked her scissors back into her apron and stood aside for Betty to try.

Louise felt a moment's dismay when she glanced down and saw the pile of silver hair on the floor. She wouldn't have much hair left when these two were done. Surely two hair dressers wielding scissors was one too many.

She went back to her magazine, preferring the triviality of the lifestyles of the rich and famous to watching what was happening to her own hair.

"Okay. I think that's as much as we want to take off," Angela said. "We'll be styling the hair with a round brush."

Louise frowned as Angela pulled out a bristly cylinder and a blow-dryer and started twisting the brush through her hair. "I don't have one of those, and even if I did, I couldn't manage to do my hair the way you do."

Angela handed the brush and dryer to Betty and then picked up what looked like a bristly curling iron still in its blister package. "You can buy this unit at the local pharmacy. That's where I got this one. It's simply a blow-dryer and round brush in one unit. Doesn't cost much and is easy to use."

And that, from the tone of Angela's voice, was that.

Betty curled and dried and Angela coached, and soon Louise could see some shape returning to her hair. And when Betty and Angela were done, she felt a moment of surprise.

Her hair shone in a smooth cap around her face, barely skimming her cheekbones. But what amazed her the most was the fact that she looked younger.

In spite of her earlier reservations, she had to smile.

"Why, Betty, that's wonderful," she said.

"I think so too," Betty replied, standing with her hands on her hips, nodding her approval. She turned to Angela. "Thanks so much for the tips. I learned a lot this morning."

Angela simply shrugged away her comment. "Cutting hair is not neurosurgery. Just common sense and a knowledge of your client." She tweaked a strand of hair above Louise's forehead and titled her head to one side as if seeing Louise from another angle. "Looks okay."

Okay? Louise thought her new hairstyle looked wonderful. What was more surprising was how rejuvenated the haircut made her feel.

"Thank you, Angela. Betty," Louise said, her smile spontaneous now.

"We'll work on the makeup next," Noralee said, gesturing toward Kim's chair. "I believe you have another client coming, Betty?"

"Martha Bevins is coming in ten minutes, though I can make it a half an hour if you need me to. I don't want to interfere with the program."

Noralee waved away her objections. "We're trying to get a realistic feel to the story, so sound and movement in the background helps achieve that."

But as Louise settled into the chair Martha Bevins came into the shop, ten minutes early.

"I know I didn't need to be here yet," she chirped, settling her tiny birdlike form into the only chair left in the waiting room, folding her arthritic hands over her oversize, box-like purse. "But I was curious to see . . ." She stopped and looked over at Louise, her tiny round glasses glinting in the bright lights. "My goodness, Louise Smith. Look at you."

Martha slowly got up. Elton had lots of time to follow her and catch her reaction. Martha's steps were the careful and deliberate movements of an elderly woman.

"What a lovely haircut. Simply lovely." Martha held her hands up in amazement, then let them drop. "You look like a . . . a princess. My, my. Lovely, lovely." She shook her head and then gave a puzzled glance at the camera. "And what is that young man doing behind there?" she asked, moving her head, trying to see Elton's face. Louise could see the camera following her movement, which made her move over more, which made the camera move over more to follow her.

She had to laugh. "He's filming for the reality show," Louise said.

"Oh my. I'm sorry. Reality show. I didn't know." Martha placed a crooked finger against her bright-red lips, then gave Louise a puzzled look. "What's a reality show?"

"A television program." Louise looked for guidance to Noralee, who simply spun her finger. Louise guessed that meant "carry on." "We're doing makeovers. I'm getting one now, and the television studio is filming. They will make a program out of it."

"Oh yes. I heard about that." Martha glanced around the shop curiously, then she turned back to Louise. "Did you read in the newspaper that there is going to be a toxic waste dump here in Acorn Hill? Aren't you worried? I am. You can get cancer from toxic waste. I heard that on the radio."

Louise patted her hand. "That was just the writer's exaggeration. What he was really complaining about was how the trash collector missed a few stops a week or so ago."

"Are you sure?" Martha asked. "I mean toxic waste, here in Acorn Hill!"

"There'll be no toxic waste dump here, I can assure you," Louise said. "The writer used that headline to get attention. If you are worried, speak to the mayor. He can reassure you."

Louise suddenly realized all this was being filmed. She said to Elton, "You're not going to use that, are you?"

Elton shrugged. "I'm afraid that's not up to me."

"Well, I guess I'm next," Martha said, giving them all a big smile. "Carry on," she said as she walked slowly back to Betty. "I'm ready for you, Betty Dunkle. No makeover for me, please. Just the usual." Clearly her worries were already forgotten.

Louise bit back a laugh and caught Noralee hiding her face behind her hand.

And Elton was filming everything.

Chapter Ten

Y ou must start with clean skin." Kim stood in front of Louise, her hands planted on her hips in a take-no-prisoners stance. "And no soap and water."

Louise held her unwavering gaze, then, realizing she was beaten, gave in. She had been arguing with Kim about the need for all the fussing before they put on the makeup. But Kim had been adamant that they go through all the skin-cleansing steps, explaining that the procedure wasn't only for her own sake, but also for the sake of the people who would be watching.

"So, we'll start with a basic cleansing step using this product." Kim held it up to the camera. "Again, this is something you can pick up at most drug stores and grocery stores that have expanded cosmetic sections." She made a cotton pad damp with the cleanser and started applying.

"You have lovely skin, Louise," Kim said, smoothing the slightly astringent lotion over her cheeks. Kim went on to discuss various exfoliants, skin toners and moisturizing creams. Louise simply put up with the regimen, knowing that soon the fussing would be over.

When Kim was done with her face, she took a package from the counter and a brush from her apron.

"The next step is makeup. I prefer to work with the eyes

first, simply because I feel they are the first thing that people will notice about you. In your case, Louise, what you want to do with eye shadow is make sure that you start with a base color that goes from your eyelid to your eyebrow." Kim pulled out a brush and demonstrated for Louise. "When you get older, your eyelids disappear, which can make your eyes look smaller." Kim drew back, looking critically at Louise, then pulled another brush out of her pouch. "This is a softer brush used for blending. We'll put the dark color on with this, making sure that you go just above the eyelid to give you a wider look."

Louise glanced again at the wide variety of brushes Kim had tucked in her pouch. "Surely I don't need to use all of those?" she asked.

"No, of course not, but it wouldn't hurt to buy yourself two good brushes for your eye shadow, one good brush for your blush and a lipstick brush." Kim gestured toward the makeup lying on the table. "Your local pharmacy sells a variety of brushes that you can use."

"And where do I store all these brushes? I barely have enough room for all my other toiletries." Louise knew she wasn't going to be buying any more makeup, but for the sake of the camera and, by extension, the television show, she pretended to go along with it all.

"You can buy a stand for them. Again, here's one that I bought at the pharmacy," Kim held up a small ceramic stand for Louise and for the ever-present camera.

Louise was getting used to the large black eye following her and was able to ignore the camera this time as she spoke to Kim.

Kim set the stand down and finished up with the eye shadow. The next step was a faint eyeliner pencil and then mascara, blush and lipstick.

Kim had turned Louise so she wasn't facing the mirror, so Louise had no idea what she was doing to her face. She consoled herself with the fact that if she didn't like what Kim had done, she could simply use the dreaded soap and water to get rid of the makeup when she was back home.

Kim leaned a bit closer to Louise, gently brushing mascara on her lashes, her lips pressed together as she concentrated on the task. One more gentle swipe and she straightened, her eyes flashing critically over Louise's face.

"Okay. I think we're done for now." She pulled Louise's smock off and lowered the chair. "Elton, what do you think?"

"Wow," was all Elton said from behind his camera as he rolled it around Louise, checking her from all angles. "She looks great."

Louise was about to brush off the comment when Kim turned her in the chair so Louise could see for herself what had been done.

She glanced at the figure in the mirror, then to Kim.

Then, feeling disembodied, she looked back at the person sitting in the chair.

It was her own reflection. And this woman was almost a stranger. Her hair framed her features in a way that drew attention to eyes that now looked, as Kim had promised, just a little wider. Her cheeks looked higher and even her mouth looked a little fuller.

"So. What do you think, Louise Smith? Were stages one and two worth it?"

Louise couldn't say anything but kept staring at her reflection. "I'm stunned."

"I like stunned," Kim said, holding up a large mirror so that Louise could see the back of her head. "Thought you might like to get a bit more of the effect."

Louise reached up and lightly touched the hair at the back of her neck. Betty, under the supervision of Angela, had cut it shorter than she was used to, but she reluctantly admitted that she liked the way her hair teased the back of her neck with gentle wisps.

Elton came closer with the camera, but Louise didn't pay much attention to him.

"This is truly amazing."

Noralee joined them and Louise half turned to look at her. "I am most impressed," she said, giving Noralee a quick smile. "I didn't think it would make this much difference."

"A good haircut and some ordinary styling tips can effect a big change," Noralee said, walking slowly around Louise, studying her from all angles. "The best part of all of this is that you can maintain this look without resorting to expensive spas or hairstylists."

Noralee turned Louise's chair around so that Louise was once again facing the camera.

"So, this is Louise Smith. She has just gone through stage one and two of our makeover project. Stage three, the clothing and wardrobe stage, will have to wait until we can assemble all of our ladies." Noralee smiled down at Louise and, reaching her own hand out to her, shook it. "Thanks again, Louise, for being a participant in our makeover program."

"Thank you. I enjoyed the process more than I thought I would." Louise was about to get up, but before she stood, she took another quick peek over her shoulder at her reflection.

"I still can't believe you did all this with only that," she said to Kim, gesturing at the makeup on the counter.

"It's all in the application," Kim said. "Thanks for participating. We'll see you in the next round."

Louise gave them both a smile, picked up her purse and her coat along the way, said good-bye to Betty and Martha Bevins and then stepped out into the warm spring air. She waited at the corner, content for the moment simply to look around. It felt like a whole new day.

"Miz Smith?"

Louise turned. Elton was standing outside the beauty parlor, his hands tucked in the back pockets of his blue jeans. He gave her a quick smile. "I might be overboppin' my bounds, but I was wondering about a young woman who was staying at the inn? She's about this tall," he pulled his hand out of his pocket and demonstrated. "Long, copper hair in a braid. Really cute."

"That would be Sasha," Louise said, recalling his earlier interest.

Elton chewed his lip a moment, as if unsure of what to say.

"Would you like to meet her?" Louise asked, taking a guess as to why he was asking about their guest.

His relieved smile showed her that her instincts were right. "I don't know if that's proper and all, but yes I would."

"I'm sure that it would be just fine. Why don't you drop by the inn? If Sasha is in, I'll introduce you," Louise said.

Elton's grin made his eyes crinkle. "That'd be great. Thanks a bunch." He tossed her a wave, then ducked back into the shop.

Confused by his interest, Louise crossed the street just as Wilhelm was coming out of his shop.

"Good day, Louise," he said absently as he pulled the door of his shop closed behind him. Then he paused and looked at her again. "You're looking especially lovely today."

"Thank you, Wilhelm."

"Have you done something different?" he asked, scratching his chin with his index finger. "You seem . . ." he turned his hand palm up, as if seeking more information.

"I just got my hair done."

"No. It's more than that." He shook his head. "I can't put my finger on it, but you look so fresh and sprightly."

Wilhelm's words made her feel even more sprightly. "Why thank you, Wilhelm," she said, a warm glow of satisfaction spreading through her. "Maybe it's the weather."

Or maybe it's the new me!

"Anyhow, you look lovely," he said. "This weather must be agreeing with you."

They chatted a moment, then he left and Louise walked on down Berry Lane toward the Nine Lives Bookstore where she knew Viola would be waiting, eager to hear how things had gone.

The wrought-iron bench by Viola's front door was flanked with pots of yellow and orange chrysanthemums, a bright and cheery note of color that made Louise smile.

As she pushed open the beveled glass door to Viola's shop, a bell tinkled gently, announcing her arrival. Louise paused inside the door and let the stimulating scent of paper and old wood polish drift into her nose. She never grew tired of the smell of new books. It promised adventure, knowledge and new places with interesting people.

One of Viola's cats strolled toward her, purring a welcome. Louise bent down to stroke his silky fur just as Viola came into the main area of the shop from her office at the back.

As Louise straightened, Viola adjusted her glasses. An uncertain smile hovered over her mouth. "Louise?" she asked, taking a tentative step closer.

"Who else would it be?"

"You look...different." Viola shook her head and walked slowly around Louise, examining her from every angle as if wanting to make sure this woman was indeed her old friend. "You look beautiful."

This time Louise did blush. No-nonsense Viola was not given to compliments, and the breathless tone of this one made Louise feel most flattered.

"I have just gone through stages one and two of the makeover program."

"You're wearing makeup." Viola made another half turn.

"That's not unusual. I've worn makeup before."

"Yes, but this time ..." Viola shook her head again. "I'm amazed how different you look. It's quite, quite ...amazing."

"You're repeating yourself," Louise said with a laugh,

"and you are exaggerating." However, wound through her discomfort was a faint appreciation for Viola's praise. Though she wasn't a vain person and had no desire to spend as much time on her looks as Kim and Betty just had, she couldn't deny a womanly satisfaction at the reaction this simple makeover had prompted.

"Speaking of exaggerating, did you read the new paper? The *Eye on the Hill*?" Viola asked.

"I haven't read it, but I've certainly heard about it. Martha Bevins was convinced that she was going to get cancer from the toxic waste dump Woody Swigart mentioned.

"Oh dear. I took it as a bit of a lark, but I can see now that it could have a bad effect." Viola wound one end of her silk scarf around her finger. "However, I am pleased that I was right about one thing, this makeover. What they have done for you is breathtaking. I wonder if they could give me some advice."

"Surely you're not one given to such fancies," Louise asked, surprised at her usually practical friend.

"I must confess that I'm a tiny bit jealous of how good they have made you look."

"Well, you know that beauty is only skin deep," Louise said. "This is all just superficial vanity."

"Maybe, but you also have to admit that you don't mind looking this good either."

Louise realized that Viola was right. After all, hadn't she only a few moments ago felt a certain pleasure because of Viola's reaction and Wilhelm's compliment?

"You're right," she conceded. "I must confess that I was surprised by the change they created."

"A nice haircut and some primping can do wonders for a girl's self-esteem," Viola said.

"We're hardly girls," Louise said with a light laugh. Then the word *girl* started a train of thought and with it, an idea.

"I'm sorry, Viola," she said, "I have to go. I'll call you tonight."

She went back to Betty Dunkle's shop. Then, when she was done there, she hurried home to Grace Chapel Inn to talk to her sisters.

"I'm thinking I just might pack up and leave on Sunday," Sasha said, pushing the toe of her sneaker against the boards of the porch. The wooden swing creaked as she set it in motion, back and forth, back and forth.

The sun was setting, slowly pulling a blanket of orange and pink toward itself, drawing the dusk in the east closer. Jane felt a chill feather over her arms. It was a bit too cool to sit outside, but after a long, cold winter, she wanted to spend as much time as she could in the fresh air.

"Why would you want to do that?" Jane asked, cradling the mug of tea in her hands. "You still have a couple of days here. I was hoping that you could come with Sylvia and me to Potterston tomorrow night."

"Two weeks didn't seem long when I won the prize, but it seems a bit long now." Sasha let a long, tired sigh drift out of her as she rocked. "I should get back. There's nothing for me here."

Jane guessed she was referring to Wilhelm. "Sasha, I'm sorry about what happened . . ."

Sasha held her hand up. "Please. I should have known that I was wasting my time. I usually am when it comes to men. It's just that I felt so comfortable around Wilhelm, and I thought because he was a little older that he might be attracted to me. I never know what to say around men my age. I'm awkward and I say the wrong things." Her voice broke and she stopped, bending her head as if hiding her shame.

Jane wanted nothing more than to hurry across the porch and give the young, sad girl a quick hug.

Instead she took another sip of her tea, thinking about what Louise had told her, thinking about Sasha around men. Though it seemed shallow, she knew that young men were often initially attracted to a woman's appearance, and Sasha spent no extra effort on her good qualities.

This evening she wore a washed-out pink shirt and a pair of unfashionable baggy blue jeans. She knew that Sasha wasn't poor, simply thrifty. But surely she could spare a few dollars for a decent wardrobe? Good clothes didn't have to be fancy, but neither did they have to be so plain and ill-fitting. Jane wasn't a vain person, but she loved dressing in fun clothes and bright colors. They cheered her up, and she wondered if a change of wardrobe wouldn't do the same for Sasha.

"Another reason I should leave is that my father probably misses me," Sasha said.

"You still live with your father?" Jane asked.

"Yes, he likes having me at home. Besides, I save a lot of money by living there. I'm putting as much as I can away."

"For what?"

Sasha shrugged. "Maybe a trip, but most of my money is put away for my retirement fund. One has to be prepared," Sasha said almost automatically. "My father often says that he wishes he had been more careful with his money when he was younger. He says he would have had more to retire on now."

"Your father is close to retirement age?" Jane asked.

"He's going to be sixty-six next year. He's been saving every extra penny he has from the time he turned forty. When my mother and father adopted me."

"What does your father do?"

"He works in a factory. Has his whole life. He has dreams of buying a condo in the Bahamas and retiring there."

Jane felt a flurry of confusion. "That sounds expensive," she said carefully.

"It is. That's why he wishes he started saving sooner, and that's also why he's been encouraging me to set up my retirement savings plan now. If I have enough money, I can do what I want when I retire." Sasha rocked a little harder. "So I need to make sure I don't spend too much money now so I can do what I want then."

Jane took another slow sip of tea and at the same time said a prayer for wisdom. "Well, I certainly admire your foresight. Of course, one's life should have balance. In this case, that would mean balancing your present and your future. If you balance things properly, you can provide for your old age at the same time that you enjoy your youth. If you spend your whole working life scrimping for your retirement, you might regret it."

Sasha gave her a puzzled look. "Why?"

"Well, because your retirement is forty years away, and you have a life to live now." Jane thought again of what Louise had suggested and realized that more than ever they needed to find a way to implement Louise's plan. She carefully set her empty cup on the porch and got up to sit beside Sasha.

"Your father has good reasons for the advice he is giving you, but you should be enjoying life as you live it. Money is only a tool. And this plan . . ." Jane faltered, struggling to find the right words to express her feelings without making it look as if she were criticizing Sasha's father, ". . . this plan is a good plan. But perhaps it puts too much emphasis on the future. To spend the most productive and most exciting years of your life denying yourself so that you can be comfortable in your old age is risky. You don't know when you're going to die, when God is going to call you home."

Jane stopped talking, realizing that she was preaching to

the poor girl. Sasha hadn't come with them to church on Sunday, and Jane didn't know if she even believed in God.

On impulse she took Sasha's hand in hers. "Does your mother feel the same way about this?"

Sasha gave her a sad smile. "My mother died two years after I was adopted. I barely knew her."

In that moment, Jane felt an immediate kinship with the young woman. "My mother died giving birth to me," Jane said quietly. "So I know what it's like to grow up without a mother."

Sasha looked away, giving the swing another push. "You said that saving all my money for retirement is risky. What do you think I should be doing with it?"

Jane thought a moment, sent up a quick prayer and then said, "I think the first thing anyone should do is make sure that they give a portion of what they've made to help others. To quote St. Francis of Assisi, 'It is in giving that we receive.' After that, I think it's a good idea to save some money for the future and for unforeseen expenses, and after that, I don't think there's anything wrong with spending some on yourself. On fun things, on travel, on clothes."

As soon as she spoke the last words, Jane wished she could recall them. She didn't want to sound like she was criticizing Sasha's style sense. In a way she admired the young woman for not being driven by fashion.

Sasha bit her lip. "Maybe you're right, but I still feel I should not have bought that expensive tea set. I only bought it because I saw it as a way to get to know Wilhelm. He seemed so nice, and I do really, really love teapots. Only I usually just buy the cheap ones." Sasha shook her head. "My father doesn't approve, so I keep them in my bedroom."

Jane stifled a flash of anger at this man who had kept his daughter so under his thumb that her one indulgence was hidden away in her room.

"Sasha, you're a grown woman. You should be in charge of your own life, making your own decisions about how you spend your time and how you spend your money."

Jane saw a flash of hope in Sasha's expression. She was about to say more when a car pulled up into the parking lot and two women got out.

Jane guessed from the blue streak in the hair of one of them that she was Kim, the young woman who had worked wonders on Louise. Louise had said that Kim and the hairdresser, Angela, were looking for a place closer to Betty's. She wasn't sure they would come.

Sasha got up, staring at Kim, who was sauntering up the walk and looking up at the inn, a large travel bag slung over her shoulder.

Angela trailed behind her, pulling a black suitcase.

"Welcome to Grace Chapel Inn," Jane said as they stepped onto the porch. "My sister told me you might be coming. My name is Jane Howard."

"I'm Kim," said the girl with the blue hair, "And this is Angela."

"I'm glad you decided to stay here," Jane said.

Kim waved her be-ringed hand. "I can put up with no cable if it means I don't have to listen to someone yelling at three o'clock in the morning."

"I can assure you there won't be any yelling here," Jane said with a smile. "I'd like to introduce another one of our guests to you. This is Sasha Webber."

Kim tossed Sasha a quick wave, then stopped, frowning as she looked her up and down. "Hey, Angela," she said, glancing over her shoulder at the other woman, who was only now coming up the steps. "Get a load of her hair."

Jane's eyes popped open at the comment. How could she say such a thing? Did Kim have no sensitivity at all?

She quickly looked at Sasha who was blushing and

looked as if she was about to bolt or cry but didn't know which to do first.

Angela joined Kim, dropped her suitcase and strode over to Sasha's side. "Oh . . . my . . . goodness." she breathed. She picked up Sasha's braid and let it fall again. "Is this your natural color?"

Sasha nodded, looking miserable. She couldn't go anywhere. She was hemmed in by the railing beside her, the porch swing behind her and the two girls in front of her.

"Have you ever seen such gorgeous hair?" Kim asked, her voice full of awe.

"Never. It's absolutely amazing." Angela sounded as awestruck as Kim was.

Jane felt the tension holding her shoulders ease.

"And that bone structure. No wonder Elton was asking about her." Kim shook her head. "Girl, you are a Sleeping Beauty, that's for sure."

"Who is Elton?" Sasha asked, her expression growing wary.

"Our cameraman. He thinks you're a cutie."

Sasha narrowed her eyes as if she was waiting for some teasing comment, but none came.

Kim gave Sasha another once-over, and Jane could see Angela eyeing Sasha's hair as if she would love nothing more than to get at it.

"You don't color your hair?" Angela asked again.

"No. Never."

"You always wear it like this?"

"Yes. It's easier to take care of," she said slowly, looking from Kim to Angela, as if still uncertain of their interest in her.

"I can show you to your rooms, if you want to get settled," Jane said, sensing Sasha's discomfort.

"That'd be great," Kim said. "But I'd like to use your

phone if I could. Need to check on the husband and kids. Your sister said that cell phones don't work too great here."

"Yes. Of course. That would be fine." Jane felt a moment of confusion. She couldn't imagine the blue-haired woman as a wife and mother.

"Great stuff," Kim said, hoisting her bag over her shoulder.

Chapter Eleven

Louise was coming out of the living room as Angela and Kim followed Jane to the reception desk.

"Oh, welcome," she said, "I'm glad you decided to stay here."

"Hey, the lure of home-cooked food and quiet neighbors was enough for me to forgo cable," Kim said, dropping her bag with a *thunk*. "This looks like a great place to stay."

"Louise, would you please sign in Kim and Angela?" Jane asked. "I have to get a few things ready for breakfast tomorrow if we're going to have extra guests."

Before Jane left, she checked on Sasha, who was back on the swing, looking bewildered. Jane didn't blame her. First she got a lecture on being more carefree, next she gets told that she's a Sleeping Beauty. For a woman who was saving for her retirement before she even had wrinkles and who barely spent any time on her looks, the new ideas would require a huge paradigm shift.

"Are you okay?" Jane asked.

Sasha glanced up at Jane and gave her a tentative smile. "Yeah. I'm okay." She frowned. "Are those women from the reality show?"

"Yes, they are. One did Louise's hair and the other her makeup."

"They did a nice job. Louise looked lovely."

"She did, didn't she?" Jane was still surprised by the transformation. The change wasn't startling, but somehow what Kim and Angela had done had given Louise a glow that enhanced her natural beauty.

Sasha fingered her hair, looking thoughtful. "I wonder if they could give me some makeup tips."

"I'm sure they wouldn't mind," Jane said, relieved that Sasha had mentioned makeup first.

Earlier that afternoon, after she and Alice had gotten over the shock of their sister's makeover, Louise had put forward her plan for a mini-makeover for Sasha. When Louise told them what a lift the haircut and the makeup had given her, she wondered if the same wouldn't help Sasha get out of her doldrums. Jane had been hoping to find an opportunity to ask her but was sidetracked by Sasha's retirement plan.

"I don't think they're busy with makeovers tomorrow," Jane said to Sasha carefully, wanting the woman to think it was her idea. The girl's self-esteem was fragile, and to suggest that she needed a makeover was like saying she had huge flaws. "You could ask."

"I just might."

"Do you still want to come out with Sylvia and me?"

Sasha hesitated. "I don't know. I'm just not good at talking to strange men."

"No strange men. It's just a fun night out. We're going to a karaoke evening."

"Is that where you sing along to music?"

"You don't have to sing if you don't want to, but karaoke can be a lot of fun."

"I suppose. But I don't know if I have anything I could go out in," Sasha said.

Yet, thought Jane. "Don't worry. You'll be fine."

Sasha still seemed to hesitate.

"It won't cost a thing," Jane said, easing away another

fear. "It's just a social evening." Joining in the karaoke did cost a few dollars, but Jane was willing to cover Sasha's costs just to get her out of the inn.

"Well, okay," Sasha said, still not convinced.

"Great. I'll tell Sylvia. Now, if you'll excuse me, I have to get things ready for breakfast tomorrow morning."

"And how did you sleep?" Louise asked as she poured Kim a cup of coffee. It was Saturday morning. Their other guest, a businessman, had eaten and gone. He was here to make connections with businesses in Potterston and was out more than he was in.

Kim and Angela had told Jane they wanted breakfast at ten, which was fine with Sasha as well.

"I don't honestly remember," Kim said, adding some sugar to her coffee. "I lay down and the next thing I know, the sun was shining in my room."

"I heard a dog barking," Angela said morosely, stirring her own coffee. "That woke me up a couple of times. Then I heard someone rattling around early this morning."

"That's too bad," Louise said.

"I thought this place would be quieter, but I never sleep well anywhere."

"What is this?" Kim asked, pointing to the warming plate in the middle of the table. It held a golden circle of what looked like an omelet.

"It's an herbed frittata," Jane said, entering the dining room with a basket of fresh buns and a bowl of halved grape tomatoes.

Angela bent closer and sniffed. "It smells odd. Why does it smell odd?"

Jane frowned at Louise, who was by now used to Angela's sullen attitude. Louise gave her a wink, and Jane nodded.

"I made it with basil, parsley, marjoram and sage as well as some spinach and fennel."

"Wow. That sounds delicious. I can't wait to try it," Kim said as Jane cut the frittata into wedges and served it with the halved tomatoes on the side.

"I think I might be allergic to parsley," Angela said, holding out her plate. "So I hope I don't break out."

"I'm sure you'll be fine," Kim said, taking a slow, appreciative sniff. "I can't wait to try this."

Louise caught Jane's eye and motioned her to the kitchen.

"Don't pay attention to Angela," Louise said in a quiet voice once they were out of earshot. "Being gloomy is just her nature. Don't take her grumbling personally."

"Glad to know," Jane said. "I was wondering what we had let ourselves in for. Is she okay with your plan?"

"Yes, she and Kim seem more than willing."

Jane picked up a plate of fruit and brought it into the dining room. Kim and Angela's silence was an eloquent testimony to what they thought of the food.

"Good morning, I hope I'm not too late." Sasha slipped into the dining room, smiling at Jane. She spared Kim and Angela the barest of glances.

"Just on time," Jane said cheerily. "I was just telling Kim and Angela about the menu. There is herbed frittata with sautéed grape tomatoes on the side, and fresh-baked buns. If you don't want anything warm, there are pineapple muffins and poppy-seed scones and fruit on the sideboard."

Sasha glanced at the frittata, then went to the sideboard and took some grapes and cantaloupe wedges. "I'm not that hungry," she said quietly as she caught Jane's surprised look.

Usually Sasha filled her plate. Cooking for her was fun because she enjoyed everything so much.

"I thought I should tell you that I'm going to be making supper for Angela and Kim while they're here," Jane said.

"We offer this service to some customers from time to time, so if you want to join us, you're more than welcome. It would save you a trip to the Coffee Shop or Zachary's."

"Thanks, Jane, I might do that," was all Sasha said.

"Did you hear that dog last night?" Kim asked Sasha. "Angela here claims the barking kept her up all night."

"No. I didn't hear anything." Sasha gave Kim another surreptitious glance and then turned her attention back to her plate.

Kim gave Jane a puzzled look. Jane waggled her hand in what she hoped was an encouraging gesture, and when Sasha looked up, she quickly covered up by pretending to rearrange the plates.

"I understand that you and Jane are going out tonight," Kim said, thankfully taking the hint.

All she got was another nod from Sasha.

"Where are you going?"

"Karaoke, I think."

The conversation was growing painful. At this rate it would take all day to segue into the area where Jane and Louise wanted to go.

"So, Sasha, what did you think of Louise's makeover?" Angela asked.

"She looked lovely."

Jane resisted the urge to roll her eyes. Could Sasha be more laconic? Usually she liked to talk. What was with her this morning?

Jane glanced at Kim, who, in tag-team fashion, took over.

"I . . . uh was wondering if you would be willing to help me out today?" Kim asked.

Jane moved to the sideboard and slowly rearranged the fruit on the platter.

"How could I do that?" Sasha asked with the first note of interest in her voice.

"Well, Angela and I are going to be working with a few younger women next week and to tell you the truth, we're a little out of practice."

Jane fought back a chuckle. Kim made it sound like she catered solely to older women, but Jane doubted that Kim's electric blue hair and multiple piercings were hardly required attire for that kind of salon.

"We are?" Angela asked.

"Oh, for sure we are."

Jane turned around in time to see Kim level Angela a meaningful look. Angela's puzzled expression faded, and Jane could see that she understood.

"Really? So what do you want me to do?" Sasha asked.

"Well, we'd like to practice some different techniques on you if we could."

Jane caught a look from Kim and realized that Kim needed some help.

"Wow, that sounds like fun, Sasha," Jane said in what she hoped was an encouraging tone of voice. "A makeup fest. Maybe I could get some tips too before we go out tonight."

"I suppose that would be fine," Sasha said reluctantly.

Jane held her breath. If Sasha could only experience a little of what Louise had, it might boost her self-esteem.

"Though I don't know anything about makeup," Sasha said, "so I couldn't tell you if it's right or wrong."

"Not to worry," Kim said. "I think we can work our way through it. If you don't mind a few mistakes."

"No. I mean, makeup does wash off, doesn't it?"

Kim waved her concerns away with a sweep of her hand. "Absolutely. Like a charm. Won't even know you had it on."

Jane relaxed. Sasha was a sweet person who was, as Kim had said, very pretty. She just had to stop hiding her light under a basket.

"Angela and I have some work to do with Noralee today,

but we were wondering if you'd be willing to sit for us after supper." Kim said.

"But Jane and I are going out tonight," Sasha said.

"That's okay, Sasha," Jane said. "Alice wants to eat early tonight, so is five o'clock for supper okay with everyone?"

"Perfect." Kim dabbed her lips with her napkin. "We can set up after that and when we're done, you can go on your merry way."

Supper was over, the leftovers put away, and Angela was upstairs, washing Sasha's hair.

"Is Angela really going to give Sasha a haircut?" Alice asked. "Won't Sasha mind?"

"She won't be taking much off. Just giving it some shape and definition around her face," Kim assured her.

Kim, Louise, Jane and Alice were sitting in the dining room waiting for Sasha and Angela to come down.

"I'm surprised she agreed to this idea," Alice said.

"I'm not," Jane said. "When she saw what Kim did for Louise, I think she might have started thinking about what makeup might do for her. I think the reason for her not wearing makeup is thrift, not principle."

"I just wish we could do something about the clothes," Kim said, spinning her rings around her finger. "That thrift-store look doesn't do anything for her."

"I like to shop at thrift stores," Jane said, trying not to sound offended.

"So do I," said Kim, "but a person doesn't have to go to the ugly section every time. I mean, there are some pretty funky things you can do if you've got a bit of imagination."

"Do you have anything specific in mind for Sasha?" Alice asked.

"Nothing too out there. Just something brighter and better fitting than what she wears now. I'm going to see what

I've got, though I don't think we're too close in size," Kim said, getting up and going upstairs.

Alice drummed her fingers on the table as she thought. She looked at Jane. "Would you mind if Kim had a look through your closet, Jane?"

"Not at all. That's a great idea."

"I wish we could get Aunt Ethel involved in this somehow," Louise said. "She hasn't been over here since the participants were chosen."

"I could phone and ask her if she'd like to help us," Alice said. "Maybe she's waiting for us to make the first move."

"It's worth a try," Louise said.

Alice got up and dialed her aunt's number. Jane and Louise could only hear parts of the conversation, but they could see from Alice's smile that the conversation was going well. Minutes later a knock sounded on the door.

"Yoo-hoo," Ethel called out as she entered the kitchen.

"We're in the dining room," Louise called to her. "Come in."

"Thanks for asking me over," Ethel said as she entered the room.

"We're glad you were able to come. We've missed you," Jane said.

With a warm smile, Ethel settled in at the table as if she had never been away.

Ethel wore a crocheted cloche. It was almost the same shade of pink as the streaks in the hair she was trying to hide. Her clear gaze fastened on Louise. "My goodness, don't you look lovely? I mean, you always did look lovely before with your silver hair and blue eyes, but oh my, that haircut really suits you."

"Thank you, Aunt Ethel."

"You should have seen her before she washed the makeup off," Alice offered. "She looked so elegant."

Ethel tugged on her hat as if suddenly aware of her own looks. "I'm sure she did."

"Would you like some dessert, Aunt Ethel?" Jane asked. "It's strawberry cheesecake."

"Oh, my favorite," Ethel said, placing a hand on her chest as if to hold her heart in. Then she looked from Louise to Jane to Alice. "I'm sorry I stayed away," she said quietly as Jane set the plate in front of her. "I was wrong. I was jealous. I thought that because I supported the makeover idea that I would get picked. I thought that having a makeover would be a lot of fun, and when I didn't get picked, I am ashamed to say that I pouted. I was wrong to be so childish."

Alice patted her aunt on the shoulder. "It doesn't matter, Aunt Ethel. We're glad that you came by to visit us."

"I couldn't find anything," Kim said as she came back into the kitchen.

Ethel glanced up and then dropped her fork. "Oh my word," she breathed when she saw Kim's electric-blue hair. "I thought I had hair problems," she said.

Alice made the introductions. "Kim is a makeup specialist who is working on the reality show. She and the show's hairdresser, Angela, are staying here. Tonight they're doing a makeover on Sasha, our guest," Alice said. "And Jane is going to get some makeup done too."

"What is the occasion?"

"Sasha, Sylvia and I are going out to Potterston to a karaoke evening," Jane said. "We're going to paint the town red."

"Well that's better than pink frizz," Ethel grumbled. She gave Kim another puzzled look. "Did you really do that on purpose?"

Kim laughed. "Yes, I did."

"Our aunt made a mistake a few weeks ago and her hair ended up in poor shape," Alice explained to Kim.

Kim got up and walked over to Ethel. "Do you mind if I have a look?"

Ethel grimaced, then slowly pulled off her hat. Kim

wasn't one bit fazed by what she saw. But then, a person with bright-blue hair is probably not easily shocked.

"The streaks are kind of cool," Kim said, "But the perm is a disaster." Kim fingered Ethel's hair. "For a true pink, you should have bleached the color out of your hair first. That way the color would have taken better."

"But I didn't want pink," Ethel fussed. "I was trying for streaks."

"And the bangs?"

Ethel sighed. "I thought if I curled them, the pink streaks wouldn't be so noticeable."

"I see," Kim said, angling her head to study Ethel's hair. "You know, that's not really my department, but I'm sure Angela could give you some help."

Ethel brightened. "Really? Could she truly help me?"

"I'm sure she could," Louise said. "But at the same time, we were wondering if you could do us a favor."

"Of course. Anything for my dear girls."

Louise glanced back over her shoulder, listening. Angela was still busy with Sasha upstairs.

"We were wondering if you'd like to help us choose some clothes for Sasha to wear tonight. We're going to go through Jane's closet for something for Sasha to borrow," Louise said quietly.

"Of course, I'd be glad to do that. I've seen her in town from time to time. She is pretty, but she doesn't try to enhance her beauty."

"We agree," said Jane, rising from the table. "I'll go and see how Sasha and Angela are faring. Then I'll join you in my room."

Jane went up the stairs with the others following behind. She went into Sasha's room while the rest continued up to the next floor.

∞

Sasha sat in a chair in front of a mirror, a black nylon smock covering the clothes that Kim wanted so badly to replace. Her copper hair hung in long, wet tendrils down her back.

Angela spared Jane a quick glance, then picked up a comb and started working on the tangles in Sasha's long hair.

"This is going to take three quarters of an hour," Angela said bluntly as she whisked the comb through Sasha's hair. She started at the bottom and all the while she worked she peppered the young woman with questions. "Have you had any hot-oil treatments?"

"No," Sasha answered, glancing up at Angela as if she felt like she had just failed a test.

"Do you always use conditioner?"

Sasha shook her head.

"Do you always wear your hair in a braid?"

"Almost always."

"Doesn't suit you," Angela said in her matter-of-fact voice, then added. "That sounds mean, but I'm trying to help. I saw that you pull your braid tight. That's not good for your hair. You can get what's called tension alopecia. Causes hair loss. It's permanent."

Sasha's horrified expression almost made Jane laugh. "I doubt it will happen overnight," Jane assured her.

"You have beautiful hair and good skin. You need to highlight that." Angela put the comb down and looked at Sasha critically in the mirror. "How do you feel about short hair?"

Sasha's gaze flew to Jane, who shook her head. Much as Angela was in charge, Jane knew Sasha wouldn't like her hair short anymore than Jane herself would.

"I . . . uh . . . don't like it short," Sasha said.

"Long then." Angela turned her chair around and faced Sasha. "One thing you need to know: I make a suggestion, then you say yes or no. You don't like it, tell me. It's your hair and you have to work with it every day. You are the boss, I'm just the hairdresser. Okay?"

In spite of Angela's blunt delivery, Jane could see Sasha visibly relax. "Okay. I understand," Sasha said. "I like my hair long."

"Good call," said Angela. "So do I. But some bangs would soften your face. And if I do bangs, I need to layer around your face. Okay?"

Sasha bit her lip and looked at Jane, who took her cue from Angela and shrugged. "Go ahead," Sasha said, then winced as Angela picked up a pair of scissors. As the scissors made the first *snick*, Sasha closed her eyes.

Jane fingered her own hair and left. She walked upstairs to her bedroom.

Half an hour later, the closet investigators entered the kitchen, laughing, each one carrying some items of clothing.

"I hope we found something that will work," Louise said.

"Kim has a good eye," Jane said, gently hanging the clothes she had been carrying over a chair. "I think we'll be able to put something together."

"I wonder how Angela's making out," Kim said. "She should be about done. I'll go check on them."

"I'm not done yet," Angela said, glancing over her shoulder. She stood in front of Sasha, hiding her from view. "You can start doing Jane's makeup while you're waiting for me."

"Great idea." Kim went downstairs and had Jane sit in the chair they had set up. Kim stood back and examined Jane critically from all angles, pulling her hair off her face. Alice and Ethel sat across from her at the table, watching. Louise went into the kitchen to make coffee.

"I don't know if this is a spectator sport," Jane said.

"We are easily entertained," Alice replied, smiling at her sister.

A knock at the front door summoned Alice, but Ethel stayed put. While Kim cleansed Jane's face with some kind of liquid, Sylvia's voice could be heard in the front hall.

Jane rolled her eyes. "Great. More tourists."

When she was ushered into the room, Sylvia giggled and sat down at the dining room table to watch.

"You're next," Jane threatened, pointing a finger at her.

Sylvia shook her head. "I wear makeup most of the time. See?" She pointed to her made-up face.

Kim pulled out her brushes and laid them on the table. "Just relax," she said to Jane. "This won't hurt a bit."

Jane did as she was told, opening her eyes when Kim said to, closing them when Kim said to, and in general feeling like a mannequin that was being painted. Twenty minutes later, Kim told her to open her eyes as she held a mirror up to Jane's face. "So, what do you think?"

Jane thought she would be prepared for what she saw. After Louise's transformation she didn't think she would be surprised.

But she was. "Look, Sylvia," she said, pointing to her eyes. "I have eyelashes."

"And lips," Sylvia said.

Jane smiled and glanced back at her reflection. "What fun. I have eyelids too."

Alice and Ethel simply shook their heads when Jane lowered the mirror. "You look lovely," Alice said.

Louise came into the dining room carrying the coffee and sighed at her sister's transformation. "You do indeed look lovely."

"Well, Miss Lovely better go get dressed," Sylvia said. "We don't want to be late."

Angela popped her head into the dining room. "You ready for Sasha?"

"You bet."

"Okay. She'll be down in a minute."

Jane was burning with curiosity to see what Angela had done with Sasha's hair, but Sylvia was right. She needed to get ready. She had picked out her outfit already. She decided on a striped oversize silk shirt over a jewel-green camisole. A tan cotton skirt, espadrilles and a matching green scarf around her ponytail finished the look.

Jane checked herself in the mirror and then went downstairs, eager to see what Kim and Angela had done with Sasha.

She was stopped at the dining room by Louise.

"You'll have to be patient," was all Louise would say.

"So? How does she look?" Jane banked her impatience and resisted the urge to peek over the swinging doors.

"You'll see," Sylvia said, but no sooner had the words left her mouth then the swinging door was opened and Kim stepped into the dining room.

"Ladies. May I present Sasha Webber."

Jane just stared. Sasha stood in the doorway as silence descended on the room.

Wisps of hair framed Sasha's face enhancing luminous eyes. Her cheeks were touched by a blush of color and her lips shone.

Her outfit—a coral-colored cropped jacket over a lacy white camisole and trim black slacks—made her look slim and fashionable.

"I think I speak for everyone here when I say *wow*," Jane said, stunned at the difference in the young woman.

"Yes, I second that," Louise said.

Sylvia, Ethel and Alice were effusive in their praise. Angela and Kim stood behind Sasha, obviously pleased with their efforts.

"So, go already," Kim said, making shooing motions. "Leave and celebrate life."

Sasha bit her lip and glanced over her shoulder at the two women.

Kim waved her hands. "No. No. Do *not* chew on the lipstick." She pulled Sasha to the table holding the makeup and quickly repaired the gloss. "This is your silver bullet," Kim said, tucking the shiny tube into the minuscule handbag hanging from Sasha's wrist. "You look divine. Now go and have fun."

Sasha gave her a tremulous smile, then glanced over her shoulder at her image in the mirror.

"Yes, that's you," Kim said. "You are beautiful, Sasha."

"Time is still marching on," Sylvia called out just as the doorbell chimed.

"I'll get it," Louise said, glancing at the clock. They weren't expecting anyone, and most of their friends came in through the back door.

She smoothed her hands over her skirt, straightened her cardigan and opened the heavy front door.

A young man stood on the step, the overhead light casting shadows on his face. His dark hair was neatly combed and his habitual five o'clock shadow was gone. Instead of a torn T-shirt, he wore a loose leather jacket over a striped shirt and neat blue jeans.

"Evenin' Miz Smith," he drawled.

"Why Elton. I didn't recognize you. Come in."

He flashed a self-conscious smile, then stepped inside.

"I was hoping to meet Sasha," he said. "Is she here?"

Louise wondered what he would think of Sasha's transformation. "She is, but she was just heading out the door."

"She was leavin'?"

"I'm sure she can see you a moment," Louise said. "Come with me."

Jane and Sylvia were standing back admiring Sasha when Louise led Elton into the room. He stopped. Louise heard his swift intake of breath, then a quiet, "Wow."

"Jane, Alice, Sylvia, Sasha. I'd like you to meet Elton De Jonge. He's a cameraman with the reality show."

The ladies all smiled at him, but Elton had eyes only for Sasha. She looked puzzled as if trying to understand why he was staring at her.

"Evenin' Miss Webber," he said, his deep voice soft. "I hope I'm not disturbin' you?"

Sasha slowly shook her head, then gave Louise a quizzical look.

"Elton has come to see you," Louise said gently. "He asked about you, and I suggested that he stop by."

Sasha looked back at Elton, who seemed to have regained his composure.

"I don't want to bother you, but . . . I just thought . . . if you weren't busy . . . maybe we could, you know, do something?"

Sasha's baffled expression slowly morphed into surprise. When she realized that this young, handsome man was asking her out, she blushed and looked down.

Elton continued to stare at her, and Louise looked to Jane for assistance.

"You know what, Elton. Sasha, Sylvia and I were heading to a karaoke evening in Potterston. We'd love for you to join us."

Elton gave Jane a grateful look. "If I'm not intrudin', I'd be happy to come."

"Not intruding at all," Jane assured him. "We'll be meeting Craig Tracy there so you won't be the only male along."

Louise saw Sasha give Elton a bemused look, as if she hardly dared believe this young man had come specifically for her.

"Let's go then. We can take my car," Jane said, picking up her jacket. Sylvia followed. Just as Sasha was about to go, Elton stepped in front of her. He held out his arm for her in a distinctly old-fashioned gesture, which made Louise's eyes misty.

Sasha's expression showed her disbelief that this could possibly be happening to her.

"Don't stay out late," Kim called out as they left. "Elton, you make sure to bring Sasha back by curfew."

Elton threw Kim an aggrieved look. He turned back to Sasha, tucked her arm tenderly in his and escorted her out the door.

Chapter Twelve

"You should have seen Sasha last night," Jane exclaimed as she whipped the batter for the crepes she was making for breakfast Sunday morning. "Every time I saw her, there were a couple of young men hanging around her. Poor Elton had to fight them off steadily."

"That would have been fun to see," Alice said as she wrapped the breakfast utensils in mauve napkins. "I'm so thankful that Kim and Angela were willing to help out. Not to mention what they were able to do for Aunt Ethel."

"What did they do?" Jane asked.

"Well, since Aunt Ethel had only permed her bangs, Angela was able to trim most of the frizz away. Then she recolored the rest of Auntie's hair. Angela told her that she would have to give herself some hot-oil treatments and deep condition every time she washes her hair. Aunt Ethel was delighted with the results."

"I was so happy that they were able to fix her hair," Louise said as she arranged daffodils in a vase. "And I'm glad that Sasha had a good time. Maybe that will help her get over Wilhelm."

"I think part of her infatuation with Wilhelm was that he paid attention to her," Jane said, setting her mixer aside. "All the attention she got last night should prove to her that she really is attractive."

Alice looked up at Louise and smiled. "And speaking of attractive, you are looking lovely this morning. Did you put makeup on?"

"Just some mascara, though I don't think I'll be wearing makeup on a regular basis. It's more work than I feel it's worth."

"You do look nice," Alice said.

"Thank you, but I still believe that, as Proverbs says, 'Charm is deceptive and beauty is fleeting; but a woman who fears the LORD is to be praised'" (Proverbs 31:30).

"True enough," Alice said, setting the wrapped utensils on a tray with the china. "And I believe you are a good example to us of the woman of Proverbs, Louise. In many ways."

"Well, she definitely does not eat the bread of idleness," Jane said, pouring another crepe into the pan. "I don't suppose crepes fall into that category."

"Crepes are a category unto themselves," Louise said. "Especially your crepes."

Jane smiled at Louise's compliment.

Louise brought the flower-filled vase into the dining room and set it on the table. The yellows and oranges added a cheery note to the room.

A soft cough caught her attention, and she looked up to see Sasha hovering in the doorway. She gestured to Louise.

"What can I do for you?" Louise asked as she joined the young woman in the living room.

Sasha wore her hair in a braid again. The same nondescript T-shirt hung over the same faded blue jeans she wore before her makeover. The only remnants of yesterday's transformation were the bangs she couldn't pull back and a smudge of mascara under her eye that she must have missed this morning. Louise was puzzled. Sasha had been so proud of how she looked.

"I need to talk to you, Mrs. Smith," Sasha said looking forlorn. "I don't . . . I don't know what to do."

Louise couldn't help the sudden jump in her heartbeat. In spite of Jane's chaperoning her, had something happened last night? "What's wrong?" Louise kept her misgivings out of her voice, trying to sound calm and reasonable.

"It's that whole Elton thing?" Sasha's voice went up at the end of her sentence as if asking a question.

"Elton?"

"I feel so bad. I don't know how to tell you this . . ."

"What happened?"

"Nothing. That's the problem." Sasha blew out her breath and ran her hands over her hair. "This sounds so dumb. We went for a walk after we got back here and he tried to kiss me goodnight. Well, I was all worried about whether I was on the rebound from Wilhelm and whether I was being fair to Elton. So I didn't let him. We had such a good time together. He wasn't at all out of line. Oh, he must think I'm an idiot."

"I'm sure he doesn't think any such thing. I'm sure he respects you," Louise assured her.

Sasha lifted her shoulders, then let them drop in a gesture of defeat. "But what about the whole Wilhelm thing? What was with that? I mean one minute I'm thinking he's the one and I like him and . . . and the next, I'm like, here's this young, good-looking guy and he's looking at me like I'm beautiful. And that's the other thing. It wasn't really me he was seeing, it was just the makeup"—she pointed to her face—"and the hair and the clothes. And what if he comes over and finds out that I'm just a faker?"

Louise listened to Sasha's words, and in them she heard a vague echo of her own misgivings. Hadn't she thought the same about her own makeover, that what Kim and Angela had done wasn't real?

But yet, her look was real. All they had done was enhance what was already there.

Louise patted Sasha gently on the shoulder. "You're not

a faker. And I know for a fact that Elton was attracted to you even before you let Kim and Angela do a makeover on you. And I don't think there's anything wrong with wanting to make yourself look a bit more attractive. It's not as if you put on a mask and a wig."

Sasha laughed. "No, I didn't do that." Then she gave Louise a shy smile. "Was Elton really attracted to me before?"

"Yes, he was. He noticed you while he was filming yesterday. Then, when I was in the salon, he asked about 'that pretty girl' staying at the inn. And you're the only pretty girl we have here, so of course he was talking about you."

Sasha blinked a couple of times, then looked away. "Really? You're not just saying that?"

"I always mean what I say," Louise said firmly.

"Okay then." Her eyes grew wide again and she caught Louise by the arms. "So now what do I do? I want to go out with him again, but if he thinks I don't like him it won't happen, will it? I don't think I should phone him. Or maybe I should?"

"Maybe you should just wait and see what he does," Louise said reassuringly. "Or, if you want, you and I could go for a walk on Monday or Tuesday to Betty Dunkle's to see what is going on, and maybe you'll have a chance to talk to him."

Sasha nodded. "Yes. That's a great plan. I like that plan." She flashed Louise a grateful smile. "And maybe I'll even put on some makeup." She looked down and plucked at her T-shirt. "And maybe buy some new clothes."

"You do what you want," Louise said, giving into an impulse and giving the young woman a quick hug.

"Is breakfast ready? 'Cause I'm sure I smelled something cooking when I came down the stairs."

"Not quite, but Jane will be done in a few minutes."

"Could I help? I think Kim and Angela are up, and they'll probably want breakfast too when they come down."

"Come on then," Louise said and escorted Sasha to the kitchen.

∽

"How do I look?" Sasha brushed her hand over her new clothes, her hands trembling as she paused at the bottom of the stairs. She wore a spring-green cotton-knit sweater and beige straight-leg pants with a pair of beige canvas wedgies. Her hair was loose, and she wore light makeup. "I don't look overdone, do I?"

"You look just fine," Louise said. "Lovely in fact." She waited for Sasha to make the next move. It had been Louise's idea for Sasha to go see Elton, so she didn't want to pressure her.

"Okay. Let's go." Sasha drew in a deep breath and walked past Louise to the front door, then yanked it open as if afraid she would change her mind. Once out in the beautiful morning sun, she quickened her pace, and Louise had to rush to keep up.

It was Tuesday morning. Sasha had finally worked up enough courage to accompany Louise to Betty Dunkle's. Louise had wanted to go on Monday. She was curious to see what Kim and Angela were doing with the other Acorn Hill women, but Sasha had practically begged her to wait.

The problem was that Elton hadn't called, so Sasha wondered if she should even bother pursuing the relationship.

But today was her last day here, and Louise, Jane, Alice, Kim and Angela had all put pressure on her to at least visit Betty's. On Monday, Sasha went to Nellie's, where she bought her outfit. Now, finally, she and Louise were on their way to where the show was being filmed—by Elton.

Betty's shop was a hive of activity. A second camera and operator had been brought in, and this operator was filming Betty and Angela washing Hope Collins' hair. Noralee stood beside the cameraman, directing the angle. Cables snaked over the floor as another young man arranged some blinding lights. Kim was bent over Nancy Colwin. This whole process was being filmed by Elton, who had his baseball cap backward on his head, hiding behind the viewfinder of his large, bulky camera.

"There he is," whispered Sasha, pointing to Elton. "He's behind the camera. He told me a bit about his work. It sounds really, really interesting."

Noralee was calling out to the young man moving the lights around. "Did you double-check the batteries in that boom mic? I'm not going to lose sound halfway, am I?"

"They're good for another four hours," the young man called over his shoulder.

"Great. We'll have a break then, and we can put new ones in." Noralee pushed her glasses back up on her head and as she turned, she caught sight of Louise and Sasha. But instead of coming over to say hello, she gave Louise a cold look and turned away.

Louise was puzzled by her reaction. The last time she had spoken to Noralee, the producer was very pleasant.

Maybe she was just busy.

Elton straightened and glanced their way. He motioned for another young man who was hovering at his elbow to take over. As he came nearer, he gave them both a tentative smile, yanked his baseball cap off his head, and tucked it into the back pocket of his jeans.

"Hey, there," he said, glancing from Sasha to Louise and back to Sasha again. "Good to see you here." He glanced over his shoulder and moved to the door leading out. "Things are nutso here right now. We can talk better outside."

Sasha looked down, suddenly shy, and Louise felt like a fifth wheel. But Sasha had insisted that Louise stay with her, so she accompanied them outside.

They stood by the building, sheltered from the cool spring breeze.

"I was hoping you'd drop by," Elton said, smiling down at Sasha. "You're looking great this morning."

Sasha brightened as she smoothed her hands over her new sweater. "Louise talked me into doing some shopping at Nellie's, and I'm glad I did. She has some nice stuff, and I wanted to, well, you know," she raised her hands, then lowered them. "I guess I wanted to look my best for you."

"You look great," he said, fidgeting. "Really great."

"Thanks," Sasha said giving him a shy smile.

"You're welcome."

"So, you're pretty busy in there doing all that filming and stuff? I imagine you've got lots to do."

"It's not bad," Elton said, leaning back against the sun-warmed building, his hands shoved in the front pockets of his blue jeans. "No different than it was yesterday, but Noralee has some bee in her bonnet this morning. She's been snapping at us ever since we came in, and it's hard to get away from her when you're working in such a tight spot."

"You won't get into trouble for coming out here?" Sasha asked, glancing nervously into the shop. "I mean, you are supposed to be the camera guy, aren't you?"

Elton flashed Sasha a quick smile. "Norm, the lighting guy, knows how to run a camera. I let him do it from time to time."

Sasha smiled up at him and Louise felt even more superfluous.

"I would like to check a book out of the library," Louise said. "I'll return shortly."

Neither Sasha nor Elton acknowledged her comment. But just as she was about to leave, the front door flew open and Noralee stormed out. She barely looked at Louise, focusing her ire on Elton instead. "What are you doing hanging around here? I pay you to run the camera, not flirt with the local girls."

"Norm can run the camera for a while. It'd be good for him. Besides, I haven't had a coffee break yet."

"We're under pressure, Elton. Coffee breaks are a luxury we aren't indulging in. Your friend can come in to watch for a little while." Noralee's angry gaze ticked over Louise, then back to her ever-present clipboard. "As for you, Mrs. Smith, there's no room in here for you."

Louise felt as much as heard the hostility directed at her. Where had that come from?

Sasha, also confused, glanced back at Louise, but Louise waved her on. "You just take your time. I'm sure you'll find the filming interesting. I'll see you back at the inn."

Noralee didn't spare another glance for Louise as she held the door open for Sasha. Louise watched them go through the glass door, still taken aback by the way Noralee had spoken to her.

Louise mentally reviewed her last conversation with Noralee but couldn't think of anything that might have caused such unveiled antagonism.

Worried, she decided to forgo getting a book from the library and thought she would visit her friend Viola instead. Maybe she could help Louise figure out why Noralee was acting the way she was.

The light tinkling of the bell announced her arrival, but as Louise entered the shop, she could see that Viola wasn't around. Usually, this time of the day found Viola either at the front desk or rearranging books on their shelves.

Louise walked toward the back of the store, the rubber soles of her shoes making no sound on the carpeted floors. As she looked into Viola's back office, she saw her friend hunched over a desk, her chin resting on her hands. She was reading.

Louise cleared her throat, but Viola didn't look up. Curious about what was holding Viola's attention, Louise came closer to the desk.

It must have been the movement that caught Viola's eyes. She glanced up, then cried out, her hand flying to her chest.

"My goodness, Louise, what are you doing sneaking up on me like that?"

"I did not sneak," Louise protested. She glanced down at the paper in front of Viola. "Whatever you're reading must be riveting for you not to have heard me."

To Louise's surprise, Viola blushed and dropped the paper she was reading.

Louise leaned sideways and read, "Makeover Madness Maddens Matron."

It was Woody's latest issue of *Eye on the Hill.* "What in the world is he talking about?" Louise asked, glancing briefly over the rest of the article.

Viola gave Louise a frown. "You haven't seen this yet?"

"Of course not. I didn't purchase the paper last week, so I'm hardly likely to purchase it this week. I don't intend to patronize the man and encourage his negative views."

Viola wrapped the end of her scarf around her finger as she glanced down at the paper again. "Well, he seems to think highly of you." Now that she was discovered, Viola handed Louise the paper.

Louise put on her reading glasses and read aloud: "Lovely Louise Smith is the kind of woman you want on your side in a fight." Louise sniffed. "What would he know?" She adjusted her glasses and read on. "She states her opinions in no uncertain terms. You know where you stand with a woman like Louise. And when it comes to the current makeover craze taking over our fair town, Louise has two succinct words to describe this trend: 'complete rubbish.' I wholeheartedly agree, which is why I am enlisting the out-spoken Louise Smith in the dissolution of this humiliating and denigrating show."

Louise gasped, shocked at his blatant campaigning and his overstated assumptions. She shoved the paper away, as if its very touch was unclean. "This is utter nonsense. He hasn't even spoken to me about getting my help. Even worse, he assumes that I agree with him."

"And you don't?" Viola asked. "I thought I heard you mentioning something along that line when the show was first proposed."

Louise thought back. "I was against the makeovers at first, but I don't remember saying that the show was 'complete rubbish,' nor do I remember even hinting that I would help him in what seems to be a campaign to stop the show."

"He also seems to think that all he has to do is state it in the paper, and it will happen." Viola took the paper from Louise and turned it around.

"Does the article give his reasons for being against the show? Not that I need to know precisely what he wrote, but I do need to understand his motives."

Viola held the paper up and read it again, shaking her head. "Doesn't look like it. Just that he thinks the show is denigrating." She laid the paper down. As she sat back in her chair, one of her numerous cats jumped onto her lap.

"How do you feel about the show now?" Viola asked, her fingers idly stroking the purring cat.

Louise lifted her shoulders in a vague shrug as she pulled her glasses off. "I have to confess that I enjoyed my own makeover. I won't be spending as much time on myself as Kim did, but I now see the advantages of wearing make up from time to time. What made it clearer was seeing what Sasha's transformation did for her self-esteem and confidence. Outward appearance can affect inner emotions. I have to confess, I experienced this effect firsthand. I'm not as against makeovers as I was."

Viola nodded as she flipped through the paper. Then she stopped and uttered a faint exclamation of surprise. "There's more than just the front-page article."

"What else could he say?"

Viola looked up, her eyebrows raised in question. "Are you sure you want me to read this?"

Louise waved her hand as if clearing away her own objections. "Go ahead, I may as well hear it all before someone else tells me."

Viola cleared her throat. "He writes, 'Guess who was seen coming out of Betty Dunkle's with a whole new look? Has Louise crossed over to the other side, or is she simply, as I suspect, trying to get an inside scoop on the goings on at Clip 'n' Curl? Her frequent negative comments about the program makes this a distinct possibility. In future issues, we'll report what her reconnaissance brings.' And then he has a grainy photo of you with your new look."

Louise massaged her temples with her fingers as if to push away the murderous thoughts running through her head. "No wonder Noralee was so angry with me," she exclaimed. "He makes me sound like a spy who is working for him. Why would he write such lies?"

Viola set the paper down. "If you read them properly, they're not really full-fledged lies," she said. "His comments are laced with innuendo and insinuation, which are the hallmarks of poor journalism. Notice how he never really comes out and says anything. He simply states a situation and then speculates in print."

"But his speculation is going to cause me a lot of problems," Louise complained. "Kim and Angela are staying with us at the inn. I'm sure they'll think I invited them to come and stay with us so that I could, as Mr. Swigart suggests, 'get an inside scoop.'"

"You only need to talk to them," Viola said in a soothing tone of voice, pushing the paper around on her desk. "I'm sure once you do that, they will realize what is going on."

"I hope so. And I hope that the people who read this paper will know as well."

"People know who you are, Louise. You were born here. Your father was a well-respected member of the community. This Elwood Swigart is a newcomer. This will pass, I'm sure." Viola toyed with one corner of the paper, smiling her encouragement.

Louise wished she had Viola's confidence. The only advantage she felt she had was that she knew the truth about her own motives. Yes, she at one time had been disparaging of the makeover, but this was an opinion expressed in the privacy of her own home. Woody had no right to broadcast her comments over the entire town.

"I feel as if I should go and talk to him," she said.

"And say what?" Viola lifted the paper up. "It looks to me as if anything you might say to him will only be misconstrued and could, in all likelihood, end up in the next issue."

Viola was right, but Louise disliked doing nothing while her reputation and character were maligned.

"Then there's nothing else to do but to simply carry on," Louise said, slipping her purse over her shoulder and getting to her feet.

"Hold your head high, Louise. You've done nothing to be ashamed of."

"Thank you, Viola. You're a good friend."

Louise left the office and walked toward the front of the shop. As she reached the door, she remembered a book she wished to order. She turned and went back into Viola's office.

Viola was sitting behind her desk, immersed in Woody's paper, an avid expression on her face. She didn't even notice Louise's reappearance.

Disappointment slipped like ice through Louise's veins. She silently turned around and left the store.

Chapter Thirteen

As she walked up Chapel Road toward the inn, Louise felt betrayed and exposed. Woody's articles were untrue. He had taken just enough of what really happened and spun her comments around to make it look as if she agreed to be on the show simply to sabotage it. How could he?

She waited for a few vehicles at Hill Street, glancing at the occupants, wondering if they, too, had read the paper and if they, too, thought she was a spy. Just as she crossed the street, she heard her name being called.

"Louise, there you are." It was Alice. She caught up to Louise and linked arms with her sister. "How about a cup of tea?"

Louise glanced at the Coffee Shop. She could see through the windows that it was almost full. Right now all she wanted was the peace of her own home and a chance to catch her breath before she had to face the town again.

"Louise, is everything okay? You look a little pale."

"I probably need to be more judicious with the blush," Louise said in a lame attempt at a joke.

Alice tugged her arm. "Come on. Let's get some tea and have a nice chat."

Louise knew that sooner or later she would have to face these insinuations. Maybe she was making more of this than she should. Maybe it was nothing, and most people would laugh off Woody's comments.

As Alice opened the door, the sound of voices gently drew Louise in. Hope was pouring coffee for some customers. Louise could see that Hope wore her hair exactly the way Betty and Angela had done it a few days previous. Her makeup was more restrained than usual, and it enhanced her features rather than overwhelmed them.

Hope finished up, turned and headed toward them, smiling cheerily.

"Good morning, Alice," Hope said, but as she looked to Louise, her smile faded and she avoided Louise's gaze. "Your usual booth is empty. Just sit down and I'll be with you in a minute."

It was easy to guess from Hope's demeanor that she had read Woody's article.

When Louise slipped into the booth, she was dismayed to see a copy of the paper lying on the table. She pushed it aside and glanced around to see who else might be reading it. Quite a few were.

"What's wrong, Louise?" Alice asked. "You seem upset. Didn't it go well between Sasha and Elton?"

"It went fine. When we arrived at Betty's shop, Elton was clearly very happy to see her." Louise stopped her account of the visit there.

"So why are you so glum?"

Louise picked up Woody's paper and handed it to Alice. She pointed to the page. "Read this and then the article inside and you'll know."

Louise could tell precisely what Alice was reading by her changing expression. "No . . . why that mean man . . . how could he?" Alice frowned at Louise, then opened the paper.

When she was finished, she pushed it away from her like it was diseased. "He wrote the article as if you're spying for him."

"And from the reactions I've gotten already, it seems that some people believe him."

"I can see that Noralee might not have been able to discount his insinuations, but surely Hope knows you better than that," Alice said.

"To me it's not a matter of knowing me, it's a matter of believing what has been written." Louise spun the paper around and glanced over the article again. "And the problem is, as Viola told me, there's just enough truth in his comments that people might believe them. Add to that my original outspoken dislike for the makeover concept, and his insinuations border on the truth."

"Isn't it defamation of character? Would people want to read that?"

"It seems that many people already are, and even worse, it seems that many of them are enjoying reading the articles."

Alice looked at the other customers and saw how many were reading Woody's paper with great interest. "I'm disappointed in the people of this town," she said quietly. "I'm disappointed that so many of them would buy and read a newspaper that treats people so badly." She tapped her fingers against the tabletop, then brightened. "I have an idea. You must tell your story to Carlene."

"What good would that do?" Louise asked.

"We'll fight fire with fire."

"I want to thank you so much for a wonderful stay." Sasha set her suitcase on the floor of the lobby beside the tote she had purchased to carry her new clothes. "This was the best vacation I've ever had. Of course, I don't go away a lot, but even if I had been on many vacations, I think this one would still be the best," she said in her familiar breathless voice. She gave Alice a quick hug.

"I'm so glad to hear that," Alice said. "We certainly enjoyed having you here."

Sasha put her room key on the desk, glanced around as if checking to see if anyone was listening, then leaned closer. "And you know what? I don't believe that Louise would deliberately spy on Noralee, even though Elton kind of does. I told him not to believe that of Mrs. Smith, that she's a good lady."

Alice appreciated Sasha's defense of Louise. "I'm glad to hear that," Alice said, taking Sasha's key and putting it away. "Louise needs all the allies she can get in this town."

"I like her a lot. Actually, I like all of you a lot. You have made a big, big difference in my life."

"Not really," Alice said with a gentle smile. "All we did was show you how pretty you really are."

Sasha turned serious. "I just hope my father understands," she said.

Alice prayed for the right words, then plunged ahead. "I think he will if you explain to him that, while you value his advice, you're a woman old enough to make her own decisions. If you want to wear makeup and go out or even have pink stripes in your hair, you should be able to do so without asking your father's permission."

Sasha nodded slowly, as if she still wasn't sure about this radical change in her life.

"I know your father loves you and wants the best for you," Alice urged, knowing that she had only a few more minutes to bolster this new Sasha. "What you must do is let him know in a loving way what *you* think is best for yourself."

"That's probably true," Sasha said. "I never let him know before."

"And he won't know if you don't tell him."

Sasha drew in a long breath, then straightened her shoulders as if stiffening her resolve along with her spine. "I will. I'll talk to him, maybe even about being on my own. Elton is going to visit me at home, so maybe he could help me find a place that I can afford."

"That would be nice if he did that."

Sasha gave Alice's hand a squeeze. "I think I like this new me, inside and out."

"I want to tell you that I always liked you, Sasha," Alice said, "inside and out, and before and after. And I want you to remember that Elton liked you that way too. Before and after."

The remainder of Sasha's insecurity seemed to slip away. "That's right. He's a really great guy, you know." Sasha bent over and pulled out the handles of the suitcase with wheels and picked up the other one, then she paused and looked up at Alice with a trembling smile. "I better get going. Thanks again for everything, Alice." Sasha blinked her tear-brimmed eyes. "You've been really good to me. You've done exactly what the plaque on your inn says. You've made me feel like I was in a place of hope and healing."

"Then we did exactly what we set out to do. And I hope that someday you will also have a place where God is at home," Alice said as she led Sasha to the front door.

Sasha nodded. "Maybe that will happen. Someday."

Alice held open the door for her, and Sasha went out and headed for her car. Alice watched as she drove out of sight and prayed that what Sasha learned from them would take root in her heart, and that Sasha would truly find God someday.

"And what prompted you to change your mind?" Carlene asked, typing Louise's comments directly into her computer.

It was late Tuesday afternoon, and Louise had found out

exactly what Alice's idea was: an interview with Carlene telling Louise's side of the makeover story. Unfortunately, the interview was too late to make the next day's paper. The article would have to wait until the following week's issue instead.

Louise had wanted to dismiss the idea entirely, but Alice insisted that they do it while Louise was still upset about Woody's column.

Now Louise was sitting across from Carlene, answering her questions about the makeover and about her reaction to Woody's article.

"I enjoyed the makeover," Louise said. "And even more, I enjoyed the way I felt. My mother always told me that handsome is as handsome does, and so I always believed that outer beauty comes from inner feelings and actions."

"Do you still believe that?"'

"Absolutely. But I also believe that we pick up unspoken clues from other people about our appearance. For instance, if I were to dress in old, dirty clothes, I know that people would treat me differently than if I wore clean and neat clothing. I believe we take in an amazing number of facts the first time we meet someone, and rightly or wrongly, we judge people on what we see. And I now believe that when I feel good about how I look, people perceive me differently than if I were self-conscious."

"So you can use makeup as a crutch?"

Louise shot Carlene a quick look, surprised by the question. "I suppose one could say that can happen."

"Do you think that's a good thing to do? Don't you believe that God loves us just the way we are?"

Louise leaned back in her chair and thought a moment, aware that Carlene had changed. She had seen Carlene do interviews before, but she would often ask predictable questions and write down the answers. Louise had never seen or heard Carlene challenge people on their answers.

"I believe God loves us just the way we are," Louise said, taking time to phrase her answers thoughtfully. Not only was Carlene going to be reading her responses, but most of Acorn Hill and, she hoped, Noralee and her film crew. "However, I don't believe people do. I'm starting to realize that it doesn't hurt to give people something positive on which to base their assumptions or their first impressions."

Carlene typed the answer, her expression giving nothing of her reaction away, which was another first for Carlene.

Louise glanced at Alice, who was also watching Carlene with curiosity. It seemed that Alice had also noticed a difference in Carlene's methods.

Carlene asked a few more questions and then the interview was over.

"Will this come out in the next paper?" Louise asked.

"Yes, it will, which unfortunately gives Woody that much longer to spread his innuendos, but none the less, it will do some damage control."

"I'm sorry I don't have an opportunity to immediately refute Woody's allegations," Louise said with a note of regret.

"Better late than never," Alice said, patting Louise on the shoulder. "People will recognize the truth when they read it."

Louise left to do some errands, but Alice remained to talk with her friends. She glanced at Carlene. "And how has business been for the *Acorn Nutshell*?"

Carlene leaned back, her wooden chair creaking as she rocked lightly. "Because the paper is mostly sold by subscription, I haven't recorded a huge drop, but last week I had a lot of unsold newsstand copies. I'm afraid that might predict a drop in subscriptions. From the number of Elwood Swigart's papers that I saw being read yesterday, my next issue will have dismal newsstand sales as well. Because his paper comes out sooner, he managed to scoop me on a couple of stories. I did an extensive piece on the area police and some lengthy interviews with law enforcement officers.

But I noticed that he also had a long piece on a similar topic."

"I don't remember reading that," Alice said.

Carlene straightened and pulled a copy of Woody's paper from beneath another pile of papers on her desk. She slipped it across to Alice. "It's on page four, the other side of the page holding the picture of Louise coming out of Betty Dunkle's."

"I have to confess I haven't read this paper at all," Alice said, flipping through the pages.

"Then you're one of the few people in Acorn Hill who hasn't," Carlene said, leaning back again, tapping a pencil against her chin. "Most of the people I talked to read his first issue and his second. I wanted to buy one, but all the places I went to were sold out. I found this one on a table at the Good Apple."

Alice skimmed over the article, complete with an unflattering photograph of one of the area's finest leaning against an older car. The caption read, "The Beater-Mobile." Following was a biting piece that discussed the broken-down cars used by area law enforcement. As Alice read she grew angry. The tone of the article was condescending and negative.

"I can't believe that people would want to read this," Alice said, flipping through the rest of the paper.

A picture of Joseph Holzmann coming out of Town Hall with a young boy was on another page with the caption, "Town councilor in training?"

"What's that about?" Alice asked, turning the paper toward Carlene so she could see it as well.

Carlene leaned forward, squinting slightly to see better. "Oh, that. It seems that Swigart thinks it was most unprofessional for Joseph to take his young nephew to a town council meeting."

Alice remembered that Joseph and Rachel were currently taking care of the boy while Rachel's sister was in the hospital. Because Rachel had been visiting her sister, Joseph must have taken his nephew to a town council meeting instead of finding a babysitter.

And now Woody, in what Alice was now recognizing as his signature style, was making it sound as if town council meetings were a joke, a casual come-as-you-are affair where everyone and his dog, or in this case child, could attend.

"Oh yes, and on the third page, under his headline 'Asleep at the Helm,' you might be interested in what he has to say."

Alice didn't want to but forced herself to see what other things Elwood had to say. "Acorn Hill says it's a sleepy town, and nowhere is that more clear than in the town council chambers. At the last town council meeting your sharp-eyed reporter didn't need to be very sharp-eyed to notice that Hank McPheeter snoozed through most of the meeting. One wonders if it's his abilities or his money that get him reelected every year."

"He is relentless, isn't he?" Alice said, shaking her head as she closed the paper. "I know Hank sometimes doesn't appear to be alert and that he can sound a bit confused, but he *is* paying attention and is very serious about his council duties."

"You can take it home if you haven't read the rest," Carlene said. "I've read it all already."

Alice folded the paper and laid it on the edge of Carlene's desk, feeling as if she should wash her hands. "No, thank you. I'm not interested in what he has to say."

Chapter Fourteen

"Here's the song list for the Sunday service," Louise said, handing Rev. Kenneth Thompson a piece of paper. "If it doesn't work for you, let me know and I'll select something else," she said.

The pastor got up from his large oak desk in his study and took the paper from Louise. He perched on one corner of the desk while his dark brown eyes skimmed over the paper. The celery-green sweater he wore contrasted dramatically with his dark hair. He always looked so neatly put together and, for a moment, Louise wondered what Noralee would change about him. Probably nothing.

"These look fine for now," Rev. Thompson said, "but yes, I will let you know if I want any changes." He looked up at Louise and gave her a quick smile. "You look nice today, Louise. Are you doing your hair differently?"

Louise was surprised that he noticed. And, if she was to be completely honest with herself, she was a bit pleased. "Thank you. Yes. It's a different style. It was part of the makeover that I participated in."

"I like it. Very nice." He nodded, but Louise could see that he looked troubled.

"Is something wrong, Kenneth?"

He swung his one foot back and forth while he pursed his

lips. Finally he said, "Yes. Something is wrong. I was hoping to let it go, but I can't. I'm not happy with what I've been hearing around town and I'm not sure where it came from. It has to do with you and this makeover program."

Louise sighed, sent up a prayer for patience and sat down in the chair by Kenneth's desk. "I'd like you to tell me what you have been hearing."

She could read the reluctance in his expression. "Please tell me," she said.

Kenneth ran his hand through his hair. "They range from comments that you were duped into being a part of this show to comments that you only agreed to participate so you could help Elwood Swigart get a negative viewpoint of the program."

Louise leaned back in her chair, frustration warring with her personal pride. "The first comment is the truth. Jane, in one of her less lucid moments, put my name into the drawing that Noralee Spracht, the show's producer, held to determine who would be on the program. Yes, I resisted at first, but after I had my own makeover, I found that I enjoyed it. In fact, I did an interview with Carlene Moss partly to dispel the rumors that I was part of helping Woody stop this program."

"But the *Acorn Nutshell* won't be out until next Wednesday, and by that time, Mr. Swigart will have had another issue of his newspaper out."

"If you want to call it a newspaper," she said with a hint of derision in her voice. "I will simply have to hope that this rumor will die out."

On Wednesday and again on Thursday, she had tried to talk to Noralee, but things had been so busy in Betty Dunkle's shop that she didn't have an opportunity. They had doubled up on the number of participants in the shop and consequently, it was a madhouse. Patsy Ley was being filmed while Angela and Betty worked on her, and in another corner of the shop, Kim was going over makeup with Nancy Colwin.

Though Kim and Angela were staying at the inn, they too had been busy. When they weren't, Louise had piano students coming in. So now it was Friday, and she still hadn't had a chance to speak with anyone from Changing Faces.

"I'm sorry to hear this," Rev. Thompson said, his frown pulling his eyebrows together. "And I'm sorry for you that you've had to deal with it. Will you have a chance to speak to any of the people on the show before they go?"

"We are supposed to have one more meeting before the final television show is taped, but I would really like to clear the air in town as well. I'm thankful the show is airing after Carlene's paper comes out."

"I don't understand people who would believe such a story about someone as respected as you."

"I'm not his only target," Louise added, describing Woody's comments about Joseph Holzmann and about Hank McPheeter. "And I have a feeling before Carlene's next paper comes out that he will have a few other people lined up in his sights."

"I wish people weren't so interested in this negative reporting." Rev. Thompson swung his foot back and forth as he drummed his fingers on his desk. Suddenly, he pushed himself away and walked to the window. "I think I know what I need to do about this."

Louise waited for him to expand on that comment, but he walked back to his computer, sat down and started typing. A faint frown line appeared between his eyebrows, and Louise could see that he was deep in thought.

She quietly let herself out, wondering what had triggered his sudden inspiration. She guessed she might have to wait until Sunday morning.

"A good name is more desirable than great riches; to be esteemed is better than silver or gold."

Rev. Kenneth Thompson looked up from his Bible reading and glanced around the congregation. "This is God's holy Word," he said as he carefully closed the Bible and set it aside.

He gripped the edges of the pulpit as his gaze took in his expectant congregation.

Usually Rev. Thompson included the title of his sermon in the bulletin that was handed out at the beginning of the service. Today, however, all that was written was the enigmatic TBA. There was no reference to a Scripture passage and no hint about his sermon topic.

He waited a moment longer and then began.

"One of the most important things we do to strangers when we meet them is to give them our name. What we may not realize is that when we do this, we give this other person power over us. From that time on, wherever we may be, this person can call out our name. And without any conscious thought, we will respond. Our name is our identity. It is also our bond. If a stranger was to come to town and use the names of some of the more well-known people in it as a reference, you would immediately draw conclusions about what kind of person the stranger was." Rev. Thompson glanced around the congregation again.

"In a small town like Acorn Hill, we carry the names of our friends and family and even business acquaintances from place to place. How we use their names will determine, in some cases, how other people see them. More important, as Christians, we carry the name of Jesus. When we misuse His name, we are poor representatives of His. When, as Christians, we misuse the names of fellow believers, we hurt both Jesus and our brothers and sisters in the Lord."

Louise knew where Rev. Thompson was going with this, and she knew why.

After Woody's latest issue had come out, Louise had received a few phone calls of support, but she also knew that other people were talking about her behind her back. However, what bothered Louise most was that she hadn't been able to speak to either Angela or Kim before they did their last makeover late Friday night and headed for their respective homes. They were due back Tuesday morning to finish the makeovers.

"The past few days," Rev. Thompson went on, eyes moving around the congregation as he spoke, "the names of some of the members of this town have been used in a cavalier fashion. I believe you know what I'm talking about."

He spoke of how easy it was to tear down, to damage and to abuse. He encouraged the members of Grace Chapel to honor the names of others—and Jesus.

When he was done, Louise walked to the back of the chapel to the organ. She noticed that a number of people who usually smiled at her averted their eyes as if ashamed.

"I don't know what I'm going to do, Alice," Carlene said when Alice stopped by the office of the *Acorn Nutshell* early Wednesday morning. "I barely sold half of my newspapers last week, and some subscribers who were due to renew haven't. I have no idea what will happen with today's issue. I would be lying if I said I wasn't worried." Carlene looked up at Alice, who could see faint lines of fatigue and concern etched into Carlene's face. The editor brushed aside a pile of papers and leaned her elbows on her old wooden desk. "You told me I shouldn't stoop to his level, but his level seems to be selling more papers than mine does."

Alice heard the note of anger in Carlene's voice and sensed that Carlene held her partially responsible for the problems she was facing with her newspaper.

"I'm sorry to hear that, Carlene." Alice wished she could come up with something more profound than sympathy. "I was counting on the people of this town preferring to have their information delivered in a positive and uplifting way."

Carlene leaned back in her chair and rubbed her right temple with the eraser of her pencil. "Oh, Alice, I still agree with you. I don't want to become a tabloid newspaper. I know that bad news sells, but I have always liked to believe that my positive view of the news is more important." She stood and started pacing around the small office. "How often do we get to read about all the good things that happen in this world? Instead, newspapers are full of divorce rates, murder statistics, accidents and crooked politicians. How many of us get to read as regularly about the self-sacrifice of children who take care of their aging parents, of parents who tuck their children into bed every night, of teachers who really care about their students?" She waved her hands as if to emphasize her comments. "These are the kinds of things I wanted to bring out in my newspaper. I like living in Acorn Hill and I like the people here, for the most part. I had hoped that people would want to read good things about the place where they live. But if they don't, then I'm wasting my time putting out my newspaper."

"I don't think you're wasting your time at all," Alice said, praying she could find the right words to encourage Carlene to keep going. "I still believe that in the long run, acting with integrity will make a bigger difference than printing the rubbish that Woody writes."

Carlene pursed her lips and folded her arms across her chest as she listened to Alice. She stopped at her desk and picked up the latest copy of Woody's paper, then threw it down.

"Why do you have a copy of that?" Alice asked.

"I wasn't going to buy it, but I believe I need to know what my competition is up to. I wouldn't be a good journalist or businessperson if I didn't try to understand why people want to buy his newspaper. So what I need to do is figure out what makes people want to read his paper and find a way to bring that element into my paper."

Alice picked it up and read the headline aloud: "Juvenile Delinquents in the Making." Then she read the article and shook her head as she dropped the paper back on Carlene's desk. "That is his take on children who were writing with chalk on the sidewalk."

"You have to admit, it caught your eye."

Alice frowned even as she realized that Carlene was right. "I'm ashamed to say that my interest was piqued, even though he ended up making a mountain out of a molehill."

"Or delinquents out of some children who were playing unsupervised." Carlene picked up the paper again and leafed through it. "Here's another example: 'Hill's Head Honcho.' It's about Lloyd being unprofessional in conducting the town council meetings." She put the paper down and shook her head. "Unfortunately, he is correct. Lloyd is a good man, but he should never have allowed Joseph to take that boy to the town council meeting, and he should speak to Hank about presenting a more alert demeanor."

"But we're talking about a child, and a man who is casual in everything he does," Alice protested. "Joseph couldn't find a babysitter for the boy. I thought Lloyd was gracious allowing him to attend. What harm could he have done? And as for Hank, his laid-back style hasn't hurt his business at all, and it certainly doesn't do the council any harm."

Carlene shrugged. "I know, Alice, but these little detours from professionalism make me wonder who's next. What's next? Imagine if Clara Horn were elected to the town council. Would Daisy be allowed to attend meetings? Much as I hate to admit it, Elwood Swigart does have a point."

"But he doesn't have to make it so maliciously," Alice grumbled, unwilling to concede. She was still struggling with forgiving Woody for the problems he caused her sister.

"Probably not."

Alice picked up Woody's paper again, determined to make her point as well. "See, what about this article on the town's traffic lights? 'Motorist Narrowly Misses Death.' All that happened is that the light flickered in the electric storm, and a driver thought it was changing and almost started into the intersection. There weren't even any other cars at the light. To me, this sensational article is another example of why you need to keep going with the *Acorn Nutshell*. You would have reported the problem to prevent something like that from happening again, but you wouldn't blow it out of proportion."

Carlene pushed her hair back from her face and sighed heavily. "Thanks for the support, but truly, if sales are as abysmal this week as they were last week, then I can't afford to stay in business much longer."

"I'm sure they will turn around," Alice said. "I just feel it."

"Unfortunately I can't make my business decisions on your feelings," Carlene said with a sad smile. "I'll have to make my decision based on sales."

"Then I'll be praying for you," Alice said. "And I'll be praying for lots of sales."

"Thanks for that." Carlene looked down at Woody's paper, then back at Alice. "Please tell Rev. Thompson that I appreciated his excellent sermon."

"You heard it?" Alice was surprised. Carlene had a casual take on faith, even though she came to church occasionally.

"Yes, I did, and hearing what he had to say gave me some hope for this community."

"Acorn Hill is a good place, and the people here are good." Alice smiled back at her, wishing once again she could do more.

Alice closed the office door behind her just as a gust of spring wind burst down Acorn Avenue at her back. Alice caught the front of her jacket and held it closed as a bunch of newspapers flew past her. The wind died down as quickly as it came, and the papers slowly settled on the sidewalk.

As Alice passed them she could see they were pages of a copy of *Eye on the Hill*.

The inn was quiet when Alice returned from her trip to town. Jane had left a scribbled note on the table letting her sisters know that she and Sylvia were going to a fabric store in Potterston and then out for coffee.

Unfortunately for the sisters, Kim and Angela had cancelled their return to the inn, choosing to go to their old motel in Potterston. Alice had encouraged Louise not to take the cancellations personally.

Two other women had checked in late Monday night and were staying until Thursday evening. Come Saturday, other guests would arrive and the inn would be full once again.

As Alice walked past the living room toward the kitchen, she found another copy of Woody's paper lying on the table. She picked it up and glanced through it again, thinking of what Carlene had told her. Yes, there was something about his paper that made a person want to read it, but at the same time, it made one feel almost dirty afterward.

Alice rolled up the paper and tapped it against her thigh. She decided to make one more visit.

Louise stood on the corner of Acorn Avenue and Berry Lane, her arms wrapped around her, holding her coat against her as she stared at Betty Dunkle's shop.

The sun was obscured by low clouds, and rain threatened. She should carry on with her errands before the rain came.

She had spent some time with Viola and then made an aimless stop at Wilhelm's. Her next stop was the library. To get there, she could either cross Acorn Avenue toward Betty Dunkle's shop and then across Berry Lane, or she could first cross Berry Lane toward the office of the *Acorn Nutshell* and then across Acorn Avenue to the library.

She knew she had to find a moment to talk to Noralee and explain to her what had really happened, but the last time she tried, the shop was busy and no one was willing to speak to her.

She didn't know if she could take that kind of humiliation again.

She made a sudden decision and crossed over Berry Lane toward Carlene's office instead. She stopped by the frosted glass door, gave into an impulse and stepped inside. Though the *Acorn Nutshell* had only come out today, she wanted to know if her interview with Carlene had generated any feedback.

As the door closed behind her, she could see that Carlene was busy with someone.

Carlene looked up from her desk and flashed Louise a smile just as the person Carlene was talking to turned around.

It was Noralee Spracht.

"I'm sorry," Louise said quietly, preparing to leave. "I'll come back another time."

"No, wait. Please don't go." Noralee got up from her chair and hurried to Louise's side. "I'm so glad you stopped by." She paused, looking a bit sheepish. "I was just talking to Carlene about our final makeover program. She's going to be covering it for the *Acorn Nutshell*, and I decided to give her an exclusive." Noralee snapped her cell phone open and shut as she spoke to Louise. She looked away, then looked down at her cell phone. "More importantly, Carlene gave me a copy of today's paper. I read the interview with you." Noralee played with her cell phone again, then looked up at Louise. "I'm sorry I didn't give you a chance to tell me your side of the story. I believed everything that I read in that other paper. I've since realized that the editor likes to distort the truth. Please accept my apology."

"Of course," Louise said reassuringly. "While it is true that I was initially opposed to the program, it is also true, as I said in the interview, that I have come to appreciate what you are doing with your makeovers."

Noralee looked relieved. "You are very gracious. Thank you."

"It's good that we had the chance to clear this up," Louise said as relief sluiced through her as well. She didn't like having Noralee think ill of her.

"I'm also glad you stopped by here for another reason," Noralee said, still fidgeting with her phone. "I want to talk to you about the last program. We've decided to have a wrap-up show for our final taping."

Louise sensed Noralee's discomfort and tried to find a way to alleviate it. "I hope you are not going to be having a swimsuit competition."

Noralee's laugh showed Louise she had accomplished her purpose. "No, you don't have to worry about that," Noralee said. "Nor will we be having an evening-gown competition. The show will simply be an opportunity to interview each one of you about your new look. We will be awarding a prize to the woman with the most dramatic makeover as well."

"When will this be happening?" Louise asked.

"I realize this is short notice," Noralee said, "but we are hoping to tape the show this Saturday."

"That sounds exciting. I would love to be there."

"Thanks. I am so happy that you can be a part of it." The sharp trill of Noralee's cell phone broke into the conversation. With an apologetic smile, she flipped it open, put it to her ear and walked away from Louise and Carlene, talking all the while.

Carlene gave Louise a quick thumbs-up. "I'm really glad you're back in the show."

Louise looked puzzled. "I didn't know I was out of it." Louise glanced over at Noralee, who was frowning now and tapping one foot impatiently.

"That's what I was hearing around town," Carlene said. Then as if realizing what she was saying, she shrugged. "Sorry. Just small-town gossip. I don't know if it's true or not."

"I guess it depends in which newspaper the rumor appears," Louise replied.

"It wasn't in either," Carlene said. "I guess not all the gossip makes it into the paper."

"It's a good thing," Louise said. She glanced back at Noralee, who was still busy with her phone call. "And I'm also thankful that I had a chance to talk to Noralee."

"When she came here to tell me that I was getting the exclusive, I asked her to read your interview. It was fortuitous that you happened to stop by."

"Considering that I was trying to avoid her by stopping by, it is fortuitous indeed."

"Or maybe it's divine intervention," Carlene said.

"Maybe," Louise said with a smile.

Chapter Fifteen

Alice pulled up to the large home at the edge of Acorn Hill and turned off her car. She drew in a long, calming breath even as she sent out a prayer for widsom and diplomatic words.

Then, before she could change her mind, she got out of the car, walked up the front path and knocked lightly on Woody's door.

She waited and looked around. Woody's home was in a newer section of town. The trees hadn't had a chance to grow as high as those in the older neighborhoods, but the area was still pretty. A young man strolled by, his head bobbing to music that was getting piped directly to his brain via his earphones.

"If kids keep that up, they're all going to go deaf."

Alice jumped, then turned to see Woody coming from the side of the house carrying a large trash bag.

"I'm sorry, did I startle you?" he asked as he set the green plastic bag on the lawn. He was dressed for yard work in a loose-fitting cotton shirt, blue jeans and leather gardening gloves.

"Yes, you did. I was expecting you to come from the house."

"It's spring. I spend enough time in my house. I figured today was a good day to work in the yard."

He looked wary, which didn't surprise Alice. After what he had written about Louise, he should be wary.

"May I help you with something?" he asked.

"I think you can," she said pleasantly, hoping that her tone and her smile would put him at ease.

"Is this a social call?"

"I hope it will be social," Alice said.

He took off his gloves and brushed some stray leaves from his denim pants as he walked toward her. "You are here to talk about my newspaper?"

"I imagine it will come up in the course of our conversation."

He laughed, then asked, "Would you like a cup of tea?"

"A cup of tea sounds lovely."

As she followed him through the house to the kitchen at the back, Alice couldn't help but look around. Jane always said you could tell a lot about people by how they decorated their homes.

Her quick glance into the living room showed masculine leather furniture grouped around a stone fireplace. Brightly colored abstract prints decorated the walls. The kitchen had ash-wood cabinets, and the furniture in the dining nook, in sharp contrast to the living room, was white wicker. A pot of silk violets sat on the glass tabletop, which also held a generous sprinkling of bread crumbs and a smear of what looked like jam.

"Sorry, I didn't take time to clean up," Woody muttered, catching a cloth from the kitchen and hurrying to the table to wipe it off. "I was in a rush to get outside."

"Here, I'll do that," Alice said, taking the damp cloth from him. "You can make tea."

Alice glanced around the cozy kitchen. The floor-to-ceiling sliding glass doors by the table filled the room with light and cheer in spite of the cloud cover. "This is a lovely home."

"I like the place. It took a bit to get the renovations done exactly the way I wanted, but in the end it was worth the fuss and bother. My next project, as you can see, is the back yard. The previous owners didn't spend much time there at all, and I will have to do a lot of work to return it to some kind of order."

He plugged in an electric kettle and pulled a pair of mismatched mugs from the cupboard and set them on the counter alongside a teapot. "What kind of tea do you like?"

"Surprise me."

Woody nodded and looked into the cupboard just as the telephone began to ring. "I know I just bought some tea from that store," he muttered, ignoring the insistent ringing of the telephone. "Ah, here it is." He pulled a tin out and set it down beside the telephone.

"I don't mind if you answer the phone," Alice said, resisting the urge to answer it herself. Louise and Jane often teased her about her inability to ignore the demands of the telephone. Jane warned her that she would break a leg one day running down the stairs trying to get the phone before it stopped ringing.

"It's no one important," Woody grumbled. "The phone's been ringing all day. I can't answer every call."

He rinsed the teapot, spooned in the tea leaves and poured the boiling water on top. "I'm afraid I don't have anything to go with the tea. Not like your sister Jane with her delicious baking."

"I'm fine with just tea," Alice said, glancing once again around the kitchen. To her surprise, the refrigerator held an assortment of pictures alongside childish drawings done in crayon and signed by the same person, Isabelle.

Woody caught the direction of her glance and smiled. "My little grandniece. She sends me letters from time to time." He walked over to the refrigerator and pulled a picture out from underneath a whimsical elf magnet. He handed it to Alice.

A wide-eyed little girl grinned back at her from the window of what looked like a playhouse. Her dark-brown hair was caught up in two ponytails high on her head.

"She's adorable," Alice said, then handed the picture back to him.

Woody smiled down at the picture again. "You have impeccable taste, Alice. I think she's adorable too." He put the picture back on the fridge, then brought the cups and the teapot to the table, gesturing for Alice to sit down.

"And how are you settling in?" Alice asked as she sat in the nearest chair.

"Fine. Or I was doing fine." Woody folded his arms on the table in front of him as they waited for the tea to steep. "The past couple of days haven't been what I'd call a high point in my life." He gave her a wry smile. "I've been getting lots of phone calls, none of them social. That's why I didn't bother to answer the phone just a few moments ago."

"I'm guessing that people are calling you about your paper?"

"Good guess." He poured the tea, handed her a steaming cup, and set one in front of himself. "I think my latest issue stepped on a few toes."

Alice blew lightly over the top of her tea, wondering what she should say to him. She remembered how upset she was with him when she had read what he had written about Louise, and now, here she was drinking tea with him.

She had forgiven him, but she knew what his paper had done to Joseph Holzmann. Alice had spoken to him a couple of days ago, and he was still upset at the implication that he was unprofessional.

"How has your paper been selling?" she asked, thinking that for now it would be best to simply show her interest in his work.

Woody gave her a shrewd glance. "Is your curiosity based on concern?"

"Why wouldn't it be?"

Woody shrugged as he absently stirred his tea. "I know that you are friends with Carlene Moss, so it wouldn't be such a leap to assume that you're asking because you want to report back to her."

"Would I have anything to report back?" Alice pressed, deciding to play him at his own game.

"Do you always answer a question with a question?"

"I understood yours to be a comment."

Woody laughed as he leaned back in his chair. "And I have another one to add to it. The paper is not doing well at all."

"I'm sorry to hear that," Alice said.

"Really sorry, or are you just being polite?"

"I am truly sorry. I don't like to see a business fail."

"I don't either. Especially when it's my business." Woody scratched his chin with a forefinger. "I thought I understood what I was getting into when I started the paper, though I have to confess putting it out is a lot more work than I had bargained for." He chuckled. "I came here to retire, and here I end up working even harder at times than I did when I was in the newspaper business."

"What were you hoping to accomplish with your paper?" Alice asked.

"Give the people of Acorn Hill something besides the bland paper they've been reading for the past who-knows-how-many years." He pushed himself away from the table, pacing around the kitchen. "I talked to people, asked questions. I did an informal survey and study and thought that the time for my paper was right. Sales were so good the first two weeks, I thought they were only going to get better, but now I'm stuck with more than half of the print run and no idea what I did wrong."

Alice wrapped her fingers around the ceramic mug and wondered how to tell him what she thought needed saying.

He hadn't precisely asked for her advice, but she sensed that this moment of confession was as close to a request as she was going to get. While she waited, she prayed for the right words.

"I think your paper served a purpose," Alice began, choosing her words as if they were flowers among thorns. "I think that you brought up some necessary points and things that needed saying." She paused, waiting for inspiration that seemed to be taking its time.

"And here comes the part where you say *but*." Woody said with a gentle smile.

"Very astute," Alice replied. "*But* you were too harsh, and I found that often you didn't deliver what the headlines promised. Or, in the case of my sister Louise, you delivered more than she had said."

Woody frowned as if thinking. "I don't remember mis-representing anything Louise had said. I laid that out fairly clearly. Louise was against this makeover program. We were both there when she made her views clear on the matter, and I simply reported that."

"Until you got to the part where she is coming out of the beauty parlor," Alice said, letting the sentence hang to see what he would make of it.

Woody frowned as if he didn't understand what she was implying.

"You made it sound as if she were spying on Noralee to report back to you."

"Oh, that." Woody dismissed her comments with a wave of his hand. "That was just literary license. That happens all the time in the line of work I'm in. We call that a teaser to make the article more intriguing."

"It wasn't true," Alice protested, "and you caused a lot of trouble for my sister."

"How?" Woody looked genuinely puzzled.

Alice was taken aback. It seemed he did not comprehend

what the repercussions of his story had been for Louise. How could she make it clear to him? Though he had lived here for a few weeks already, she knew that he could not yet understand how things worked in Acorn Hill.

"You used to work in an office, didn't you Woody?" Alice asked, struggling to find the angle that he would be able to connect with.

"I did. For many years."

"And in that office there were cliques and groups and politics that management really had no control over, yet you all came to work every day and worked together whether you wanted to or not, correct?"

"That's right." Woody's frown showed Alice that she hadn't made the connection yet.

"Think of Acorn Hill as a larger version of an office. So many parts of our life intersect with the same people. We shop together, we worship together, we sit in the Coffee Shop together. The biggest difference between Acorn Hill and an office is that in an office when the workday is over, people leave the office and go home to separate lives. That doesn't happen in Acorn Hill. Our lives and businesses, our failures and successes are so intertwined that it's often hard to separate public from private. People take things personally. So when you made it sound like Louise was disdainful of the makeover program, that she was spying for you, the people who were in favor of this makeover program took it personally. Ridiculing something they thought was a good idea insulted them. And friends of Carlene thought Louise was a traitor." Alice stopped, then laughed. "My goodness, lately I feel as if all I've been doing is delivering sermons."

Woody shook his head. "That's okay. I'm beginning to understand."

"You live in this town now. You are going to be a part of it. I think you need to know how it works."

"Is that why not many of my last issue sold?"

"I don't know the precise reason. I can't speak for everyone in this town."

"Did you buy an issue?"

"I have never bought a copy of your paper."

"Why not?" Woody leaned forward, resting his elbows on the table.

Alice toyed with her cup a moment. "Part of my reason was loyalty to Carlene. I didn't think a town the size of Acorn Hill needed another newspaper. My other reason was I didn't like the content or tone of your paper."

Woody nodded as he drummed his fingers against the top of the table. "What would you change about it?"

"I don't know. I'm not a newspaper person. I just know what I like and don't like."

"That doesn't give me much direction." He sighed heavily. "I still believe that there are things that need to be said, and I don't believe Carlene is saying them. The town council isn't run as efficiently as it could be, the town's garbage collection is sporadic, some bylaws should be tightened up. But even though Carlene was at the same meetings that I attended, she never brought up these points. I got a call from Mayor Tynan. He told me that he did not allow personal relationships to affect his decisions, and he did not appreciate the insinuation that he did. He also assured me that McPheeter only looks like he's sleeping during the meetings. However, he did say that he might have been wrong about letting the boy attend the meeting. That surprised me and affirmed my reasons for starting my paper: to add a critical voice so that things are not overlooked."

"Have you talked to Carlene?"

Woody frowned. "About what?"

"About what you think needs to be said."

"No. I haven't."

"Have you considered running for town council?"

"You said yourself this town was a tight-knit community. I wouldn't stand a chance."

"You won't know until you try. Besides, people were buying your paper for a while. Obviously something was making a connection."

Woody nodded slowly, as if absorbing her comments with each nod. "I suppose that's true."

It was getting late. Alice had made this visit on impulse, but she did have other things to do. She finished her tea, picked up her cup and brought it to the counter.

"Leaving already?" Woody asked. "You just got here."

"I'm sorry, but I have an afternoon shift at the hospital and I have chores to do at the inn before that."

"Thank you for coming by," he said, slowly getting to his feet. "I appreciate the visit. Will you come again?"

Was it Alice's imagination, or did she hear a hint of loneliness in his voice? For a moment she put herself in his shoes. He was from the city and new in a town where most people, as she said, knew each other fairly well. In spite of his confidence and occasional bluster, she imagined that he could be lonely.

"Why don't you come to dinner at the inn tomorrow evening?" she said on impulse.

The enthusiasm on his face showed her she had made the right gesture. "I'd love to come. Thank you."

"Then we'll see you at six-thirty." She gave him a quick smile and left.

As she drove back to the inn, she prayed for the right words to break the news to Louise. But her sister was forgiving, and she was fairly sure that once she explained the situation, Louise would come around.

∞

"Absolutely not." Louise snapped the tea towel to get the wrinkles out and with a few deft moves, folded it into a neat square. "I will not have that man sitting at the table with us."

Alice was taken aback by her sister's refusal. "He did before."

"Yes, he did. And he betrayed our trust." Louise snapped another towel with a flick of her wrists and gave Alice a meaningful look. "I've been publicly humiliated by him and though in my heart I've forgiven him, I don't trust him. And you shouldn't either."

Alice thought of the fleeting sense of loneliness she saw in Woody's expression and wondered if she was being too sympathetic to him. Louise had often teased her about having a soft heart, and while Alice knew this was true, she also felt that it was better to err on the side of kindness than of caution.

"I'm sure he's sorry for what he did to you," Alice said carefully.

"Then why hasn't he called to say so?"

"Maybe he doesn't know how."

"If he's sorry, he'll learn how." Louise stacked the folded tea towels and brought them to a small linen closet just beside the pantry.

Alice smoothed out a wrinkle in a face cloth she was folding, taking her time while she tried to think of how to change Louise's mind. She was sure once Woody was in their home and Louise saw him face-to-face that she would feel more comfortable with him.

Louise returned and started folding the towels with Alice. They worked in silence for a few minutes, then Louise stopped.

"You're trying to find a way to make me change my mind, aren't you?"

Alice gave her an innocent look, but when she met Louise's eyes, she conceded defeat. "Yes, I was."

"Why?"

Alice sighed as she shook out another towel. "I think he's lonely."

Louise said nothing to that and Alice, sensing that she was weakening, pushed a little harder. "He's new in this town, Louise. He doesn't know anybody and I think he's trying to fit in."

"By writing the things he does?"

"Okay, I'll concede that maybe he was harsh and he drew some bizarre conclusions, but he comes from a big city and big newspaper background. Maybe he's had to write like that to get people's attention."

"It's a nasty way to do so."

"I agree."

"You would think that Mr. Swigart has spent enough time in this town to understand its culture." Louise smoothed out the towel and laid it neatly on the stack.

"But it takes time to get to know people in a small town. And you have to admit that not all the things he wrote about in the paper were wrong . . ."

Louise gave Alice a sharp look, and Alice changed her tack.

"He is lonely, Louise, and I think he's having trouble entering the community."

Louise was quiet, and Alice caught a softening in her sister's blue eyes. She pressed the advantage. "Just think how much of a change you had to make when you moved here from Philadelphia, and what Jane had to adjust to when she moved here from San Francisco. People didn't entirely approve of our bed-and-breakfast when we first started it, but now they're okay with it. But we had the advantage of Father being so well respected and well loved by the town."

Louise looked at her sister with affection. "And, of course,

Jane and I had the extra advantage of your glowing reputation as well."

Alice felt a flush of embarrassment warm her cheeks. "I've never done as much as Father did."

"You've done wonders," Louise said quietly. "And now you're working one again. You've spent time with Woody, and I'm sure you've encouraged him. Now you are trying to ensure that he feels welcome here in spite of what he's done. You are a real example to me of Christ's love in action." She sighed as she pulled another towel out of the laundry basket. "So, given all that, yes he can come for supper, but I have to confess that I still have my reservations about him."

"Of course, I understand. Thank you, Louise, for allowing him to come to dinner. I appreciate that."

"Elwood Swigart is the one who should be appreciative," Louise said huffily.

Alice sensed it was time for a change in the subject. "What's the next stage in the makeover program?"

"On Saturday we will have a final taping of the show, and on the following Friday it will be aired."

"Are you nervous?"

Louise shook her head. "Now that Noralee understands what happened, doing the taping will be an easier proposition than it might have been."

"I think you could win. Kim and Angela made you look so beautiful."

"You haven't seen what they've done to the other particpants," Louise said.

"I'm looking forward to the program. I'm so excited that we can watch it being filmed."

The ringing of the doorbell Thursday evening announced the arrival of their first dinner guest.

Louise was still upstairs getting dressed, and Alice was

on the phone with Ethel, who had called to make sure of the time she was expected. Alice had figured that Ethel's presence would lighten the mood of the dinner. Rev. Thompson was also invited.

As Jane walked to the door, she glanced over the dining-room table. The silverware shone, the china gleamed. She had lit the tapers just a few moments ago, and the glow of their flames on each side of the simple bouquet of roses added an elegant touch.

Woody was standing in the doorway when she opened the door. "Come in, come in," Jane said, opening the door wider and standing aside.

She gave him a quick smile, hoping it looked sincere. When Alice told her of her plan to have Woody come for dinner, Jane matched Louise with her initial objections. She felt that he had betrayed their trust by what he had insinuated about Louise. At the same time, she also trusted Alice's tender instincts and knew that forgiving was part of what they were required to do. In this case, Alice was right in having him over.

Woody stepped inside. "It smells wonderful in here, Jane," he said, hanging his coat on the antique beech coat-rack just inside the door. He tugged on the cuffs of his shirt and adjusted his cardigan, then glanced around, avoiding Jane's gaze. "I miss staying here. It's quiet in my home."

"Are all the renovations done?" Jane asked politely as she escorted him into the living room.

"Most of them. There are a few minor things that need to be fixed yet, but they can wait." He sat down on the edge of the couch and glanced around. Then he took a deep breath and settled back. "Are any of your current guests going to be joining us for dinner?"

"No. They've already left for the evening."

Woody nodded and glanced around the living room again. "From my research I understand that it is difficult to keep a bed-and-breakfast financially viable. How do you and your sisters manage to do so?"

Jane hesitated, wondering why he was interested in how they ran their business. "We manage just fine," she said firmly.

Woody frowned. "I know what you charge and I have some idea of the overhead and the day-to-day costs. I find it hard to believe that you stay solvent on that."

Jane couldn't help the niggling suspicion that his questions raised. She decided to be as direct as he. "And why do you want to know?"

Woody blinked, caught off guard by her question. "I'm simply curious, that's all." He then nodded slowly. "I'm sorry. I can see that you are questioning my motives. I guess it's simply a newspaperman's natural inquisitiveness."

Jane acknowledged his apology with a nod, though she still didn't trust him.

Woody opened his mouth to say more, but the doorbell rang again.

"I'll get it," Louise called out as she came down the stairs.

Jane could see Woody glance over his shoulder to the door at the same time Louise opened it.

"Good evening," Jane heard Louise say. "Come on in."

Then Woody's eyes opened wide when he saw who was escorted inside.

Carlene Moss.

Chapter Sixteen

"Jane, how do you keep coming up with such unusual and wonderful dishes?" Ethel said, glancing over the table. "I know this is pork roast." She indicated a platter of roast slices fanned out like a deck of cards. Glistening baby carrots dotted with flecks of basil and garnished with parsley surrounded the slices, adding a splash of color. "But it has a deliciously different aroma."

"It's apricot roast," Jane said, setting a basket of fresh dinner buns beside the roast. "I marinated the pork in a mixture of apricot preserves and cider vinegar, then basted the roast with the marinade as it cooked. It's something a little different."

Alice brought in two more serving dishes. One bowl held a medley of oven-roasted vegetables, including asparagus, zucchini, summer squash and red peppers seasoned with parsley, cilantro and basil. The other held yellow- and red-skinned baby potatoes.

Woody inhaled leisurely, eyes closed, as if savoring each individual scent. "This is overwhelming."

"I agree," said Rev. Thompson who was seated across from him. "But I've been spoiled by being a guest here often, so I'm not as surprised as I might have been."

"What do you usually make for yourself at home, Woody?" Alice asked as she sat down at the table.

"Macaroni and cheese," he said, laughing at himself.

"That's hardly healthy." Carlene glanced at his waistline as if looking for evidence of his poor diet.

Woody held her gaze. "I don't always do what I should, I'm afraid."

"We know that," Carlene said with a touch of asperity.

"But I can be taught," he replied.

Carlene didn't give an answer to that. Instead she turned to Ethel. "Your hair looks very nice," she said.

"Angela fixed it for me." Ethel looked from Woody to Carlene as Louise sat down at the table. Louise cleared her throat and quiet descended.

"We usually begin our meals with prayer," Louise said, looking around the table, the glow of the candle reflected in her blue eyes. She let her gaze touch each person, but Woody was looking down. "Pastor, would you mind saying grace?"

Rev. Thompson smiled at her, nodded and bowed his head. He waited a moment as if gathering his thoughts. "Thank you, Lord, for good company and good food. Thank you, Lord, for the community that we are a part of. Help us to build each other up and to encourage each other so that we may each be salt and light in a seeking world. Bless this food that you have so richly provided. May we share our abundance with those in need. Amen."

Another moment of silence followed his prayer, and Louise found herself adding an extra prayer for forgiveness and patience with Woody. Though she thought that she had forgiven him, seeing him in person made her realize that sometimes forgiveness had to be extended to others in stages.

Jane started serving, and soon the soft hum of dinner conversation filled the room.

"I understand you come from Boston, Rev. Thompson. How did you choose to live in Acorn Hill?" Woody asked.

The pastor swallowed a bite of pork roast. "I appreciated the peace and quiet of the community but also recognized that there would be certain challenges here that I wouldn't face in a city congregation."

"Some of those challenges being . . . ?"

Rev. Thompson dabbed his mouth with his napkin and glanced around the table. "Acorn Hill has a rich history and established families that have their own peculiar traits and strengths. My challenge is to show the people that God loves them unconditionally, that they can separate themselves from any history that might be painful."

"History such as . . ." Woody said, opening his hand as if to encourage further confidences.

Louise knew what Woody was doing, and she suspected all he wanted was more material for his so-called newspaper. She was about to interrupt when she saw Alice shake her head as if to remind Louise that Rev. Thompson could hold his own. Instead she listened and tried to enjoy the delicious meal.

"We have families in our community and in my congregation who have had disputes, major and minor, about things like property lines or barking dogs. Stories get passed on about unequally distributed inheritances—always a touchy issue." He took another bite of roast and smiled at Jane. "What a wonderful flavor," he said. "It's almost a sweet-and-sour."

"Thank you. When I first read the recipe I wondered about the combination, but it turned out well."

"I think this one should be added to the Grace Chapel Inn cookbook," the pastor said.

"Are you still compiling one?" Ethel asked.

Louse felt herself relax as the conversation turned to the as-of-now phantom cookbook that Jane referred to when guests asked for recipes. Rev. Thompson had neatly avoided giving any specifics to Woody, and the discussion took a more pleasant turn.

"Pastor, I wonder at your reference to family inheritance," Woody said, returning to the conversation that Louise had thought safely ended. He was tenacious, she had to give him that.

"How did you resolve that problem?" Woody asked.

Rev. Thompson took a sip of water, and as he set his glass down, Louise saw a vague smile play around his lips. "I wasn't referring to any specific problem. I was speaking in generalities, which, I'm sure you'll understand, is necessary in my calling."

"Of course, of course," Woody said. "I apologize. I wasn't trying to pry, merely trying to understand this place I'm living in."

"Carlene is a longtime resident," the pastor said. "You might want to ask her some questions about Acorn Hill."

Woody glanced across the table at Carlene, who seemed to be ignoring him.

"I could tell you a few stories, that's for sure," Ethel piped up. "I've been here quite some time. I know where the bodies are buried."

Louise gave her a warning look, and for once Ethel got the hint.

"But of course I don't know if I should tell you, in case what I say ends up misquoted in the next issue of your paper," Ethel added.

Woody gave her a pained look. "I understand your reluctance." He paused, setting his fork on his plate as he cleared his throat. He looked across the table at Louise. "Louise, if I may have your attention?"

Louise's heart flipped over once as she looked up at him. What was he going to do now?

He held Louise's gaze for several moments. "I think it would be appropriate, while I am in your home and visiting with your family and friends and"—he glanced quickly at Carlene—"in the presence of a fellow newspaper editor, that

I formally apologize for the embarrassment and hardship my newspaper article has caused you." He lifted his shoulders in a shrug. "I guess I was still coming at my stories from the point of view of a city editor. In that job I seldom got to see the people we wrote about face-to-face, as I have in this town. Louise, I extend my most sincere apologies. I will be putting something more formal in my next edition as well. I didn't understand the consequences for you of what I had done."

Louise held his gaze and, in spite of her earlier misgivings, felt that he was being sincere. "I accept your apology."

"Thank you. As always, you are gracious and kind." He then turned to Carlene. "So, Carlene, it seems that I have to learn about the long memories in my newly adopted town. Would you enlighten me as to how this town works?"

Carlene pushed a potato around on her plate and then looked at him again. "People in Acorn Hill are like people everywhere. They have good and bad in them. The town is not a perfect place to live, but it is a good place to live. I usually prefer to showcase the positive."

"I've noticed that. But surely there are points that need to be raised? Stories that should be exposed?" Woody glanced around the table to include everyone in the discussion.

"I think there are enough people in this town who take care of that."

"The town gossips, you mean?"

"We have a few, yes."

"So I suppose I need to talk to them if I want to find out about the underbelly of this town."

"Our town is made up of flawed people," Louise said quietly. "Every place bears the taint of sin and injustice, there's no doubt. And if you go looking for the negative you will find it, I'm sure."

"So you don't think I should go looking?" Woody asked Louise.

"I don't think anyone should exaggerate what he finds," Louise said.

Woody nodded as if absorbing her comments.

"What made you choose to live in Acorn Hill, Woody?" Jane asked, turning the conversation back to him.

"I wanted to move to a small town, to get away from the city."

"You were looking for peace and quiet?" Jane continued her questioning.

"Yes. But I got bored quickly. That's why I started the paper. However, one of the first rules of journalism, or writing for that matter, is to know your audience. I'm afraid I miscalculated on that score. But now I want to learn about Acorn Hill."

Carlene held his gaze as if testing his sincerity. "And why would you want to do that?"

Woody returned her look, then smiled. "The sales of my newspaper have dropped substantially, and it seems that I have offended many of the people of this town," he turned his hand toward Louise, "including Louise, as you so eloquently and diplomatically pointed out in the latest issue of your paper."

Carlene acknowledged his compliment with a graceful nod.

"I broke the rule," he continued, "I don't know this town. So, until I do, I'm folding the paper."

"Why would you do that?" Ethel cried out. "It was fun to read something more provocative for a change." She caught a look from Jane and frowned back at her. "Well, it was. You have to admit that *Eye on the Hill* wouldn't have sold as many issues as it did initially if other people didn't think that paper was interesting too. You do a fine job, Carlene, no doubt about it, but I like reading another viewpoint on the things that happen in Acorn Hill."

Rev. Thompson was smiling as he listened to Ethel.

"Why don't you tell us what you liked about the paper," he suggested.

Ethel took a quick bite of her vegetables, then dabbed her pale-pink lips with a napkin. "First of all, I thought he brought a fresh view to some of the things that go on. I know that Lloyd didn't like the idea of Joseph bringing that boy to the town meeting, even though he had a good reason. Of course, it wouldn't have been too hard to find someone to take care of the child, but Joseph can be stubborn that way. Likes to take care of his own, he kept telling Lloyd. So Lloyd let him and he ended up looking silly. When I read that article, I thought, good for you, Woody, for telling it like it is."

Louise stifled a smile at Ethel's use of the outdated phrase. "So do you think that made a difference, Aunt Ethel?"

"I think the story helped Lloyd explain to Joseph that he shouldn't do that again. He felt that he had someone on his side." Ethel turned to Carlene. "You probably wouldn't have said anything against Joseph. I mean, he does put ads in your paper from time to time for his antique store."

"He *is* a regular customer," Carlene murmured.

"Did you agree with Woody on Joseph's bringing his nephew to the town meeting, Carlene?" Louise asked.

Carlene seemed to ponder the question. Then she straightened, as if making up her mind. "Yes, I would have to say so. I didn't at the time because I didn't want to ruffle any feathers."

"But that's our job," Woody put in. "We need to speak and ruffle for those who don't dare. It's our duty. Our calling."

Carlene frowned. "Do you really believe that?"

Woody leaned forward, his eyes bright. "Yes, I do. Okay, maybe I didn't exactly get everything right, but at the same time you have to admit I brought up things that not everyone dared to say. For instance, I know that there were people other than Louise who were against having the makeover program filmed in Acorn Hill. But because so many people were in favor, I found they didn't dare speak up. My paper did that for them."

"What about what you did with Louise?" Rev. Thompson put in, his quiet voice and gentle manner taking any possible sting out of his question.

Woody had the grace to look embarrassed. "I made a mistake there. It's a throwback to how we used to report things at my old newspaper. Maybe not as ethical as it could be, but you must admit, effective."

"It certainly created a stir," Louise said, feeling her emotions toward Woody thawing.

Woody looked around the table. "I know now that most of my problems seem to stem from not understanding the nature of a small town. But I'm seeing a good part of it here. I want to thank you for inviting me, Alice. And you also must believe that I'm sincere when I say I want to find out more about this place. I've seen good things as well as negative."

"Oh, there's quite a bit of both here," Ethel chimed in. "I could tell you stories . . ."

"However, now might not be the time," Louise said quietly but firmly. While the Howard sisters found most of Ethel's stories entertaining, Louise also knew that Ethel might not know when to quit.

"Probably not, but I think you're making a mistake in folding your newspaper, Woody," Ethel said, forking the last potato from her plate. "You people are forgetting his story about the garbage that has been piling up. Lloyd has been after that new garbage man for weeks to get his act together. Woody's article gave the man the push he needed. So that was a good thing,"

"Thank you for your support, Mrs. Buckley . . ."

"Please. Call me Ethel," she said.

"Thank you, then, Ethel. But I don't believe this town has sufficient population to support two newspapers."

Carlene tapped her finger against her chin, her lips pursed. "But Ethel, you do believe that there's a place for what he has to say?" she asked.

Ethel nodded, dabbing her lips. "Absolutely. And I know that there are people in town who feel the same. He wasn't always right, but he brought up things that I never read in your paper. Things you might not feel comfortable bringing up about your longtime neighbors and friends."

Carlene acknowledged her comment with a nod. She then turned to Woody. "Much as I hate to admit it, I think Ethel has a point. I wonder if you would be interested in working together instead of against each other in this."

"What are you proposing?" Woody asked.

"How about writing a weekly column in my paper? We could start with that and see how people receive it."

"That's quite a comedown from a full-fledged paper to a single column."

"You did say you were going to cease publication. I would think that a weekly column is a step up from no writing at all." Carlene gave him a wry look, and Woody smiled.

"What kind of column would you be looking for?"

Carlene lifted her hand in a vague gesture. "We could discuss the content. Your paper brought out some important points. These could be covered in your column, only under my editorial direction."

Woody gave her a knowing look. "You don't trust me?"

"I have a paper to run and a community to live in and, I might add, so do you."

"And you'd be getting your name around," Ethel added helpfully.

"I think that sounds like a workable solution," Louise put in before Ethel could continue.

"It would definitely add another viewpoint to the *Acorn Nutshell*," Carlene said. "And that might not be a bad thing."

"Having another writer would also help share the work-load," Alice added. "Woody could cover the political aspects of Acorn Hill, leaving you to do what you do best, and that's the human-interest stories."

"I think that could work," Carlene said, nodding her approval. "What do you think, Woody?"

Woody looked around the table. "I think I may have found a way to salvage some of my dignity."

"And add another page to Acorn Hill's history," Ethel said.

General laughter followed that remark, and as the dinner wound down, people moved from the dining room to the living room for coffee and tea and more conversation.

Woody asked more questions about Acorn Hill. As they chatted, Louise discovered that he was truly interested in the town. He just had to learn how to show his positive side and, she suspected, Carlene was just the person to help him.

Chapter Seventeen

Louise, are you ready?" Jane called through Louise's bedroom door. If they didn't get going soon, they were going to be late. Noralee had given specific instructions to be at the Harrisburg television studio on time.

"That's the fourth time you've called her in ten minutes," Alice said as she and Jane waited in the hall outside Louise's bedroom. "I think you're more nervous than she is about this show."

"Well, it's not every day that my sister gets to be on television. And we might be, too, you know."

Alice frowned. "How do you figure that?"

"Maybe it's like the Oscars. The winner is announced, then the camera pans to the audience and the viewers get to see the friends or family hugging and kissing the winner before he goes up to get the prize." Jane's eyes sparkled in anticipation. "And then maybe someone important in Hollywood is watching and they'll see us and think '*Her*—I want *her* for my next movie.' That could be exciting."

"Have you been dipping into the cooking wine?" Alice asked, a teasing note in her voice.

"No. I was just indulging in a fantasy that I had as a girl walking the streets of Acorn Hill, hoping that maybe someone would 'discover' me."

"As if they would come here looking for future talent," Alice said.

"Hey, we've had parts of a television show filmed here. This could be the beginning of something really big."

"It's just a small, local network," Alice reminded her as she slipped her sweater on.

"You're not seriously going to wear that are you?" Jane asked, looking slightly horrified at Alice's outfit.

Alice smoothed her hand over her denim skirt. "Why not?"

"You look like you're going to hoe corn," Jane said.

"I'm not the one trying to catch the eye of a hotshot movie director," Alice teased Jane.

In contrast to Alice's subdued outfit, Jane wore a leaf-green shirt and black pants belted with a matching green-and-black silk scarf. A jeweled pin sparkled from her hair, which flowed in shining waves over her shoulders.

"I'm not either," Jane said, flashing a quick smile at her sister. "Just being me." She flicked back the sleeve of her shirt, frowning at her watch. "If she doesn't hurry up, Sylvia is going to give up on us and go on her own. Louise, are you coming?" Jane called.

"Yes, I'm coming." Louise came out of her room. She wore no makeup and her hair looked freshly washed.

"I should take a picture of the 'before' for posterity," Jane said with a grin.

"You should not," Louise said as she closed her door. "You are looking lovely, though."

"Thank you. This is my future-Hollywood-star outfit," Jane said, winking at Alice and ignoring Louise's puzzled look. "And now, we need to take care of the current star of Acorn Hill." She bowed and waved her hand with a theatrical flourish. "Madam, your Toyota awaits you."

Louise laughed and led the small procession downstairs and out into the warm spring sunshine. "It seems a shame to spend most of this day indoors," Louise said, glancing around the yard.

"I hear your pain," Jane said. "I'm giving up a perfectly good gardening day to accompany Your Majesty to the ball."

Louise just laughed and got into the car. Alice had been elected driver and Jane copilot. Soon they were on their way to Sylvia Songer's home. Aunt Ethel had already received two tickets to the final taping via Patsy Ley and left with Lloyd well before now.

"What do you think your chances are?" Sylvia asked once they were on their way.

"It doesn't matter to me," Louise said. "I'm just going to have fun."

"Which means we're going to have fun," Jane said, glancing back at her sister. "Are we allowed to whistle and stomp when you win?"

"No, you are not," Louise said firmly. "I am not going to win, and even if I did, I would hope that you would behave in a manner suited to your years."

"You're only as young as you feel," Jane sang out as Alice turned onto the interstate. "And today, I'm feeling positively youthful."

They chatted as the scenery slipped past them. Jane liked car rides and today, with the sun shining and a measure of anticipation hanging over them, she truly felt in high sprits.

"Aren't you going a little fast?" Louise said to Alice.

Alice glanced at her speedometer and then at the traffic that seemed to be zooming by. "Oops, I'm a bit over the speed limit, but the other cars are going even faster."

"If you get stopped, we'll be late for sure," Louise fretted.

"We won't get stopped." Just as Jane spoke, a state trooper zipped past them, lights flashing. "See? He's on his way to catch some criminal who was driving much faster than we are, which, by the way, just about everybody is."

"He might be waiting."

Jane glanced at her sister again and gave her a reassuring smile as she recognized Louise's worrying for what it was. Nerves.

"You'll do fantastic," Jane said confidently.

When they got to Harrisburg, Jane checked the map and calmly pointed out where Alice had to go. She could tell that it had been some time since Alice last drove in busy city traffic.

"The next turnoff, to the left, should get you to the studio," Jane said and Alice switched lanes to get into the correct one.

Soon they saw a sign sporting the call letters of the studio. Alice drove slowly over the parking lot and pulled into an empty spot. "I guess we're not the first ones here," Jane said as she looked around. "I just hope we're not the last ones."

"We're right on time," Louise said. "I'm feeling a little stressed about the speed at which we traveled. I hope it doesn't show."

Jane winked at Alice, who was smiling at Louise's fussing. "You look fabulous already, Louise, and Kim and Angela haven't even had a chance to get at you yet."

"Indeed," Louise said as she got out of the car.

Sylvia, Jane and Alice followed her across the parking lot to the large studio.

Once inside, they paused, looking around the slightly cramped reception area. A woman sat behind a waist-high C-shaped divider that was emblazoned with the call letters of the television station. She wore a headset attached to a telephone. She glanced up at them when they came in and held up a finger indicating that she would be with them shortly.

While they waited, Jane looked around and caught a glimpse of an anchorman whom she saw on the newscasts from this station.

He looked taller than she expected. He stopped to talk to a woman, another television personality who had her own regular early morning show.

Feeling starstruck, Jane pulled her attention back to the receptionist, who was finishing up her conversation. She turned to them. "What can I do for you?" she asked looking bored.

"We're here for the reality show," Louise said.

"Name please?"

"Louise Smith."

The woman nodded and pulled a list from another part of her desk. "What about the rest of you? Are you all a part of the show?"

"Audience members."

"You have tickets?"

"Yes."

"Well, you'll have to wait until we're ready for you. That's not for another two hours."

Jane wondered what they were supposed to do in the meantime but presumed that this was not the woman's problem.

"Do we come back here then?" Jane asked.

"Sure. You want to be in Studio 2." She looked at Louise. "Mrs. Smith, you are to meet Noralee in the greenroom in ten minutes. She'll tell you what to do from there."

Louise glanced back at Jane and the rest. From the pained look on her face, Jane could see that she would have preferred to be with them.

"Just go and let them make you beautiful," Jane said, making a shooing motion with her hands. "You'll be fine."

Louise glanced back at the receptionist, who was writing something up for her. She handed it to Louise, then pointed away from her. "Go down this hall and take the first hall to the left. There'll be a sign."

Louise shifted her purse on her arm. She started walking even though Jane knew she didn't understand the young woman's instructions.

Jane looked at Alice and Sylvia. "I guess it's coffee and tea for us until it's time for the show to start."

"If you come early, you'll get the best seats," the receptionist told them.

"Thanks for the tip," Jane said. On the way out they met Hope Collins, who was by herself.

"I'm so nervous," she said, catching Jane by the arm. "I don't know if I can go through with this."

"Of course you can," Jane said, patting her on the arm. "You'll be fine."

Hope drew in a deep breath. "Is Louise here already?"

"Yes. The receptionist sent her to something called the greenroom. I guess Noralee is going to meet her there."

Hope fidgeted with the handle of her purse, avoiding their gaze. "I was hoping I could catch her alone a moment. I need to apologize for my behavior the other day. I didn't realize that she didn't know what Mr. Swigart had written about her in the paper. That wasn't kind of him to make it look like she was working for him."

"I would agree," Jane said quietly. "But I think things are settled between Woody and Louise now. He was over for dinner the other night. He apologized to Louise, and he and Carlene had a nice long chat."

"His last paper didn't sell so well," Hope said.

"Woody realizes the mistakes he made. Carlene offered him a job doing a weekly column for her paper."

Hope brightened. "Really? That would be kind of neat. I mean, even though he wasn't always exactly truthful, he did have some good points."

"Carlene admitted that herself," Sylvia put in. "I think it's a good match. Carlene can tone Woody down, and Woody can challenge Carlene to stick her neck out a bit and put some more zip into her articles."

Alice nodded at Sylvia. "I hadn't thought of it that way before, but I think you could be right." She turned back to Hope. "We shouldn't be keeping you. Good luck on the show."

"Thanks, Alice. I'll be looking for you in the audience."

"I doubt you'll see us," Jane said. "You'll be so busy modeling all the lovely outfits they have picked out for you, you won't have time for us mere mortals cheering from the sidelines."

Hope laughed, then hurried into the building, the large glass door closing behind her.

"Well, I guess we're at loose ends for a bit," Jane said. "Let's go exploring."

"Let's not," Alice said firmly. "I don't want to get lost in traffic or somewhere in this city. I'm sure we can find a nice little restaurant close by."

"Alice, where's your sense of adventure?"

"I haven't had to use it for some time now and don't intend to today."

Two cups of beverages later, they were back at the television studio with a number of other people, some of whom were strangers to Jane. As they waited to get in, she gathered from the conversation around her that some of these people came to tapings on a regular basis. For them it was like going to a movie or a play, just another form of entertainment.

Jane, Sylvia and Alice followed the group of people down the long hallway to a set of open double doors.

They stepped inside a cavernous room that was cool and semidark.

The half-circle stage in front of the audience was so bright, it hurt Jane's eyes. She made her way to the empty chairs set out in concentric semicircles, each row higher than the previous one.

As the crowd settled into the chairs, Jane sent up a quick prayer for Louise, who was already nervous enough. All along she had thought it was going to be an intimate show, but from the size of the studio and the number of people who kept streaming in, that was not to be.

She caught a glimpse of Ethel, Lloyd and Pastor Ley, but they didn't see her. She also saw June Carter and wondered who was taking care of the Coffee Shop.

"This is so very exciting," Alice whispered as she sat in the upholstered chair. "It's like a play, except we know the people in it."

Jane looked around, surprised at how bare the actual studio was. She could see wires and cables and exposed pipes behind and above the backdrop of the stage. Above the stage hung long squares that Jane suspected had something to do with controlling the sound.

Four cameras were rolled into place while they watched. Another man with earphones and a clip-on mic was shouting directions at someone on the other end while he simultaneously waved at the person who was moving microphones into place.

It was controlled chaos, Jane thought, watching with bemusement. She wondered what Louise was enduring backstage.

A tall figure wandered onto the stage and chatted idly with one of the cameramen.

"Isn't that Stu, the announcer from the other shows?" Alice nudged Jane with her elbow.

"Looks like it, though his face looks odd."

"Probably all the makeup he has to wear for the television." Sylvia said. "Oh, look, look. There's Elton," she whispered excitedly, pointing to one of the cameramen who was busy adjusting something on the large camera.

"Where?" Jane leaned forward as if to see better.

"Behind the second camera to the left."

"Do you think Sasha's here?" Alice asked.

"Maybe." Jane looked around, craning her neck to see

better, but in the half light of the audience area, it was hard to make out anyone's face.

Then, as if on a prearranged signal, everyone began rushing around and calling things out. Two men were shouting orders both to the people on the floor and into their clip-on mics.

Jane thought of the last few minutes, sometimes seconds, before a meal was ready to be served. No matter how often you made the meal or how prepared you were, some details could only be taken care of at the last minute.

Then the hostess of the televised program, Marnie Bredeson, came onto the set. While she was talking intently to the man with the clipboard, a young man fitted her with a mic, and before he was even done, another woman touched up her makeup and hair. All around, people were yelling and calling out the time left.

Over all of this, a man was calling out instructions to the audience, telling them to follow the cues that would tell them when to clap and when to be quiet. Two of the many cameras were directed at the audience, and Jane guessed that they picked up audience reactions.

Another woman made some last-minute adjustments to the set as more people scurried around with light meters. Then Marnie took her seat and turned to one of the cameras, her smile fixed in place as a young woman on the floor counted down the time.

Some music started playing. Jane felt a surge of excitement.

Alice leaned closer to Jane. "This is so amazing," she whispered.

"I don't know about you," Jane whispered back, her eyes still on the brightly lit set, "but I'm ready for my close-up."

Alice gave her a playful poke in the side and settled back to watch.

The hostess introduced herself, and while she was speaking, the audience was prompted to applaud.

As the applause died down she introduced Stu, who strode onto the set to more applause. He made himself comfortable beside her.

Marnie gave him a quick smile, then began to speak again. "As you all know, we've been spending time in Acorn Hill, a small town on the edge of Lancaster County, Pennsylvania." she said, her manner breezy and conversational. It was as if she was sitting in a living room, chatting comfortably with good friends.

She and Stu took turns explaining how the filming had happened and what had taken place so far. As she spoke, pictures of the various participants before their makeovers were flashed on a large screen behind them.

"What we're going to be doing tonight is to vote on a makeover winner."

More applause was solicited, and the audience obliged.

"We're going to meet all the contestants and get their reaction to the makeover and in general simply get to know them."

"That sounds like fun," Stu put in with a smile.

"Definitely," Marnie said. "So now, will you join me in welcoming our first contestant, Hope Collins."

The sign came up, but many members of the audience were ahead of the game and were already applauding. It was obvious that many of the audience members were residents of Acorn Hill who had come to cheer on their women.

Hope looked radiant. Her hair had been given some coppery and brown highlights and was cut in a reverse page-boy with the front sections of her hair sweeping her jaw line, longer than the back section.

She wore a cropped olive jacket and wide-legged pants.

She looked beautiful.

Marnie welcomed her to the show and proceeded to ask her questions about who she was and where she came from. Hope was quiet yet articulate. Jane could see that Hope's job as a waitress gave her the kind of people skills needed in an interview like this.

"So what did you think of what they did with you?" Marnie asked as "before" pictures were flashed up on the screen.

Hope twisted around a bit to see better and smiled at the images shown on the screen. "I was fairly happy with how I looked before, but what I liked the best was that I got some really practical makeup advice. It was also fun, however, to try on clothes that I wouldn't have to pay for."

"Did you choose your outfit?"

Hope looked down at her jacket and ran her hand lightly over the pants. "No. I would never have picked this. First of all, the color isn't one I thought would look good on me, nor did I think I could wear this style, but it seems to have turned out okay."

"You're too modest. You look fantastic." Marnie looked to the audience, holding out her hand for more applause, which was quickly granted. "Don't you all think she looks fantastic?"

The applause went on longer than it was supposed to, Jane guessed, because Marnie's patient expression looked a bit forced. Finally she started speaking and the noise from the audience died down on its own. Marnie asked Hope a few questions about her job, then talked for a while about her new look.

"Do you think you're going to keep it up once you're back in Acorn Hill?" Marnie asked.

Hope self-consciously touched her hair and shot a nervous glance toward the audience, which, Jane was sure, she couldn't see through the glare of the lights. "I hope to. The customers in my restaurant often teased me about always fooling around with the color of my hair. I just wasn't satisfied with that." She returned her hand to her lap. "But now I really like how it looks, and the style is easy to take care of.

I'm really thrilled with what Kim, Angela and Betty Dunkle did for me."

"Wonderful." Marnie asked her a few more questions about her shopping habits, then passed her on to Stu, who didn't seem to have much to ask her at all.

Jane noticed a man standing out of camera shot but within Marnie's line of sight holding up his hand and counting down. Without missing a beat, Marnie started speaking to Hope again, wrapped up the conversation, introduced the commercial break and announced their next guest, Louise Smith. She held her pose and her smile a moment as someone counted down again, and then she hopped off her stool.

Bedlam ensued as people swarmed over the set. Stu was complaining about his lapel mic. Marnie wanted a drink of water, and then her lipstick needed to be redone. Through all of this Hope was looking confused. Another person came up to her and ushered her off the set.

"Will the whole show be like this?" Alice asked, sounding puzzled. "It seems so, well, haphazard."

"Like I was thinking just a few moments ago, it looks like me working in the kitchen moments before I'm about to serve a complicated meal. Organized chaos."

Alice acknowledged this. "I suppose."

Sylvia, who was sitting beside Alice, leaned forward to get Jane's attention. "Do you think Marnie knows anything about Woody's newspaper article about Louise?"

"I can't see why she would want to bring that up. It's old news and has been dealt with." But even as she spoke the words, Jane felt a niggling worry. *It would make for an interesting conversation.*

"Oh, look," Sylvia said, suddenly sitting up and waving. "Elton sees us."

Jane and Alice looked in the direction she was pointing in time to see Elton waving his hat at them. His wide grin was a welcome sight. He pointed toward the group of people behind him, and when they looked in that direction, they saw Sasha.

She looked very pretty. Her hair was loose, and she wore a pink-and-green patterned shirt with darker pink slacks.

"I hope we can see her after the show," Jane said.

They chatted a few more moments, then the lights came up again. Marnie and Stu came back on the set and took their seats, looking at the camera while someone counted down.

"I think I would get tired of people always telling me what to do," Alice whispered.

"It's the price you pay for fame," Jane said. "Oh, we're supposed to applaud again." She obediently clapped.

Then, when Stu introduced Louise, her polite clapping became enthusiastic. She only just resisted the urge to whistle as Louise walked onto the stage. Her sister was far too elegant for something so raucous.

Louise wore a pink-checked jacket and skirt with fringe trimming the edges of the lapels and the hem of the skirt. She wore ivory pumps and pale hose. Her hair gleamed silver in the overhead lights, and her eyes looked extra bright enhanced by makeup.

Jane could see Louise scanning the audience, her eyes blinking against the glare. Jane waggled her hand but was fairly sure Louise could see nothing.

"Wow! Look at our sister," Jane said in surprise.

As with Hope, the applause kept on a little longer than it should have, and during it Jane heard an enthusiastic yell and glanced around to see where it came from.

Three rows behind and five seats over, she could see Woody applauding enthusiastically, his smile even wider than Elton's. As Jane watched him, she thought back to his stay at the inn and had a flash of insight. Woody, in his own peculiar way, was fond of Louise and possibly attracted to her.

She wondered if the contentious article he had written

about her was some perverse way of getting her attention. She felt a moment's sympathy for him. She thought of a comment a friend of hers in San Francisco would make after yet another disastrous date: "Behind every blustering man hides an insecure boy."

She turned her attention back to Stu and Marnie, who were now taking turns speaking.

They followed the same format they had with Hope. Pictures of Louise lit up the big screen and when one came up of Louise, Jane and Alice, Jane felt an elbow dig into her side.

"Look. That's us. On television," Alice murmured.

"And so very close up," Jane said with satisfaction.

Stu asked Louise a few questions about the inn to put her at ease. Then he folded his hands on his lap. The grave look on his face gave Jane pause. Somehow she knew what he was going to ask her.

"I find it interesting that *you* are on our program today," Stu said, giving Louise a forced smile.

Jane closed her eyes a moment and said a prayer for her sister. They should have guessed this might come up.

"I presume you're referring to a piece written about me in one of our local papers," Louise said.

Jane recognized the frown on her sister's face. The prim turn of Louise's lips was a look Jane had been on the receiving end of from time to time. Especially when Jane had said something inappropriate.

"Why, yes, I was," Stu said, momentarily surprised by Louise's taking the lead.

Louise turned to face the camera, looking completely in charge of the situation as she carried on, ignoring Stu, who looked as if he wanted to say something more. "Yes, there was a time that I was against the idea of enhancing one's appearance. I admit that. I was of the opinion that putting on makeup was like telling God that He made a mistake. But

I've seen what enhancing outward appearance can do for one's inner soul. We are, unfortunately, a society that makes judgments based on looks." Louise turned back to Stu. "I'm sure, Stu, that you would have had a harder time getting your job if you had a wart on the end of your nose."

Stu involuntarily touched his nose, which caused a titter of laughter from the audience.

He opened his mouth, but Louise carried on.

"I was pleasantly surprised at the difference a bit more attention to one's outward looks could make in one's opinion of oneself and, by extension, the world's opinion. My mother was a righteous and God-fearing woman who taught me modesty and simplicity. She also taught me that to take care of my outer appearance was to give a certain respect to the people I encounter in my day-to-day activities."

Jane leaned forward, drinking in Louise's words. Because their mother had died giving birth to her, Jane had never known her mother. She took in any reference to Madeleine Howard with pleasure.

"Our mother was also a woman who, if given advice on how to maintain a respectable look, would have taken it."

"So you are no longer opposed to the idea of putting on makeup and parading in front of a television camera?" Stu asked.

Louise gave him an indulgent look. "I would hardly call sitting here chatting with you *parading*. But no, I no longer have a problem with the idea of a makeover or of spending time on one's looks. It is, as with many of the things that are enjoyable in life, a matter of balance and what is appropriate."

"So the one-time spy has been converted," Stu said with relish, as if he had been waiting to use that line ever since Louise had come on stage.

Jane heard a light gasp from beside her. "Oh no," Alice whispered.

Louise simply smiled and held his gaze as if waiting for him to say something worth responding to.

Stu blinked, then glanced at Marnie, who returned his puzzled look with one of her own. Jane could see a man on the sidelines motioning to Stu, frantically spinning his finger in a circle. She guessed the silence was creating a momentary awkwardness, and the man was motioning him to move on.

"Well, I see that I'm right. I'm glad about that." He drew in a quick breath, trying to get back on track as he glanced around the studio.

Jane saw a movement by one of the cameras and glanced over in time to see Elton grinning as he moved his camera away from Stu.

"Mrs. Smith, I understand that you have a music degree," Marnie put in, taking momentary control of the interview. "What are some of the things you are able to do with that in a town like Acorn Hill?"

Louise spoke about her music students and how she played the organ at the church. While she spoke, Jane could see Stu regain his composure.

He took over again and the interview went smoothly. At the end, he was his jovial self again. "I'm glad you could join us today, Louise Smith," he said as, on cue, he wrapped up the interview. "And I wish you all the best in the voting round of this program."

"Thank you for your time," Louise said, rising from her chair like a princess who had just deigned to grant a somewhat doltish peasant an interview. "And thank you for your good wishes." She gave him and Marnie a regal nod and swept off the stage, still smiling graciously.

"Way to go, Louise," Jane said, her voice heavy with relief as she sagged back against her chair as the lights came up for the commercial break.

"She handled herself well," Alice responded.

Jane wanted to get up and go look for Louise but suspected that her sister was in a room somewhere, waiting for her next appearance.

The rest of the interviews were uneventful but also interesting. Jane found out that Patsy Ley harbored a secret ambition to become a Broadway performer, and Nancy Colwin worked quietly among the area's sick and infirm.

The rest of the women interviewed looked equally impressive. Each of them had been outfitted in something unique yet not outlandish. Jane recognized the pink dress Patsy Ley wore from Nellie's store, and she realized that the producer had truly created a small-town makeover experience by using all the resources available to the women of Acorn Hill. Jane was pleased.

And then, after all the interviews and the breaks, came the moment everyone was waiting for.

The women came back on the stage one by one and were reintroduced as their "before" pictures filled the screen again. But this time, they stayed up as each woman took her place in the row of chairs that had been set out during the final commercial break.

Stu was all smiles as he explained the procedure that had been used to determine the winner of the program.

A group of judges had been formed from various industries. They judged the women on how dramatic each one's change had been.

Stu and Marnie stood to one side at a podium, looking at the women as they spoke, reassuring all of them that no matter who won, they all looked fantastic.

"So, Marnie, maybe you could explain again for the sake of our studio audience and our viewers what the prize is."

"I know it's something I wouldn't mind getting," Marnie said, holding up an envelope. "Right here I have the airline tickets with an open date that will take the winner to . . ." she paused while a picture of chalk-white beaches and turquoise-blue water came up on the screen behind the women, "the Bahamas. The winner will receive an all-inclusive one-week stay at a resort of her choice and, on top of all of that, one thousand dollars in spending money."

A few gasps went up from the studio audience, and even Jane found herself wishing momentarily she had put her own name rather than Louise's into the box.

"Stu, I think we should put the ladies out of their misery and open that envelope you have in your hands."

Stu waved it around. "I don't know, Marnie. I'm tempted to leave and take this with me."

"Do that and I'm sure you'll have the lovely ladies of Acorn Hill chasing you down," Marnie joked. Jane imagined Nancy Colwin and Louise running after Stu demanding the prize and almost laughed aloud.

"But instead I'll open it and announce that the winner of the contest is . . ." he pulled out a card, looked at a camera and smiled broadly. "Hope Collins."

Hope's mouth literally fell open as the news registered, and a wild applause broke out spontaneously through the audience. Then she squealed and turned to Patsy Ley beside her, who caught her in a tight hug.

She got up and made her way to the podium, her hand on her chest, looking around as if still trying to absorb this while the applause from the audience went on and on.

"Congratulations, Hope," Marnie said, giving her a quick air-kiss once the noise died down a bit. Stu gave her a manly hug and then propelled her to center stage.

Hope looked around again, shaking her head as people started clapping again. "I can't believe this," she said over the noise of the audience. "I feel overwhelmed. I don't even have a thank-you speech prepared because I didn't think I would win." She paused a moment, gathering her thoughts as she looked down at the envelope Stu had given her. She pressed her hand against her chest again, still looking stunned as the applause wound down again. Then she spoke. "I do want to thank Betty Dunkle and Noralee Spracht and Kim, Angela and Nellie for helping me look the way I do now, and to Louise Smith for helping me realize that beauty is more than makeup and hair and clothes." She drew a quick breath, then looked past the cameras at the audience. "I want to thank my town of Acorn Hill for coming out and supporting all of us. I feel honored and humbled by winning this. I know winning doesn't make me more beautiful than any of the other women who were in the program. Maybe I just had the most improving to do."

Laughter followed this comment. She waited a moment, then continued. "But thanks again. I feel like I don't deserve this, but thanks to the station for giving me this prize. I'm going to enjoy having people pour my coffee for a change."

After more laughter, Stu and Marnie, on cue from the man with the clipboard, shook her hand and ushered her back to the rest of the women as music swelled. They waved to the audience as the house lights came up and the camera panned the applauding audience.

"Here's our chance, Alice," Jane said, nudging her sister with her elbow as two of the cameras swept the audience. "Look elegant and refined."

"How about we just smile and wave," Alice said.

"Sounds like my kind of reaction," Sylvia said, doing exactly what Alice suggested.

Stu and Marnie were talking to the rest of the women as the audience slowly filed out.

"I guess all we have to do now is wait for Louise," Jane said as they made their way to the main floor.

"I thought that was way cool," a breathless voice called out. Sasha fluttered up to them, excitement all over her face. "I think that's so neat that Hope won the trip. She'll have fun, not just because she's supposed to, but because I'm sure she just will."

Jane and Alice gave Sasha a quick hug, and Sylvia said hello just as Louise joined them.

"Oh, Louise, I'm sorry you didn't win. You look so beautiful," Sasha enthused, catching Louise by the hand.

"You are looking lovely yourself," Louise said with a bright smile. "I'm so glad to see you again."

"Well, you ladies were so good to me, and I really, really appreciate everything you did." Sasha glanced over her shoulder at Elton, who was talking intently to another man. "Elton is a wonderful person, and I'm so happy to have met him. He's so sweet and kind."

"It's good to hear that, Sasha," Louise said. "You'll have to come and visit us again at the inn when you have the time."

"I want to do that. Badly," Sasha said. Then she looked over her shoulder again. "I should go, but I'll keep in touch. I'm so, so glad I could talk to you for a bit. You make sure you have a good trip back home."

They waved at her as she left, and Louise said, "She's so sweet. I'm glad that she's happy."

"So, I'm sure, is Wilhelm," Sylvia said, which made the three of them chuckle.

They chatted for a bit, sharing impressions of the show and their reactions.

Jane became aware of someone hovering in the periphery and glanced over to see Woody Swigart. She welcomed him over with a wave, and he accepted the invitation.

"I just want to congratulate you on a dignified interview," Woody said to Louise.

"Thank you for that, Woody," Louise said.

"I'm sorry I was the one to put you in that position," he said, "but you handled it graciously."

Louise gave him another smile. There was an awkward moment, and Woody left.

"Are you finished here?" Jane asked after awhile.

Louise looked over her shoulder at the empty set, then at the clusters of people still dallying, some of them from Acorn Hill. "Yes. I'm done. I'm tired of people hanging around me and fussing with me, and I'm ready for a cup of coffee."

"Sounds good to me," Sylvia said. "We can go back to that place we went to after we dropped you off."

"Excellent. Let's leave."

"Hope Collins, off to Bermuda," Jane read aloud, snapping open the *Acorn Nutshell* to the second page and laying it out on the table.

It was a quiet Wednesday morning at the Coffee Shop. The inn had three couples as guests over the weekend and they had just checked out that morning. To treat themselves after the busyness of so many guests, Alice, Jane and Louise had gone to the Coffee Shop.

"That's hardly news," Louise said, giving Jane a quick look over her reading glasses. She was working on a crossword puzzle, a new and welcome addition to the *Acorn Nutshell*.

"That's the problem with a newspaper in a town this size," Jane said, smiling. "By the time something happens here, putting it in the newspaper is almost redundant."

Alice took the second section of the paper and started reading, then chuckled. "Listen to this: 'Announcing the demise of *Eye on the Hill*, a result of poor financial health. Woody Swigart wants to thank those members of Acorn Hill who took the time to correct him and thanks those who supported him through the paper's tenure. Starting next week, however, Mr. Swigart will be a regular columnist in the *Acorn Nutshell*. He looks forward to connecting with the good citizens of the town through that venue.'" Alice looked up at her sisters. "So, I guess it's official."

"It's too bad in a way," Jane said, turning another page. "He did have a way with words."

"Not a way I think anyone would want to emulate," Louise said, erasing an entry in the puzzle.

"Well, he certainly knew how to get the town's attention," Jane said, "Even though he didn't seem to be able to capture yours, Louise."

Louise gave Jane a long-suffering look. "Now why did you bring that up?"

"Because I'm your sister and I love you and I think it's kind of cool that you can still snag the attention of a man."

"I wasn't seeking his attention, I can assure you."

"Of course you weren't," Alice put in. "But you have to admit, it was flattering."

Louise gave both her sisters an indulgent eyebrow wiggle and returned to her crossword.

Jane glanced at Alice and gave her a wink.

"She liked it."

"Absolutely."

But Louise didn't rise to the bait, and Alice and Jane returned to reading the news of the past week in not-always-so-sleepy Acorn Hill.

Which was just the way they liked it.

Sweet-and-Sour Apricot Pork Roast

SERVES SIX TO EIGHT

3 to 4 pounds pork loin roast
2 tablespoons olive oil
1 6-ounce package dried apricots
1½ tablespoons cornstarch
1 cup heavy cream

Marinade:
½ cup water
1 14-ounce can beef broth
½ cup apple cider vinegar
1 cup apricot jam or preserves
1 teaspoon salt
¼ teaspoon pepper
1 medium onion, chopped
1 medium carrot, chopped
1½ tablespoons pickling spice in cloth bag

Combine marinade ingredients in a saucepan and simmer for fifteen minutes. Cool completely.

Place roast in a bowl just large enough to hold meat and allow marinade to cover it. Cover and refrigerate for twenty-four hours.

Preheat oven to 450 degrees. Remove meat from marinade and pat dry. Heat oil in a pan and sear roast on all sides.

Remove pickling spices from marinade and discard. Pour marinade into baking pan, place roast in center of pan and cover pan with aluminum foil. Place in oven. Reduce temperature to 350 degrees and roast thirty-five minutes per pound or to an internal temperature of 170 degrees. Remove foil for the last thirty-five minutes.

Remove roast from pan and keep warm. Strain juices into a saucepan, reserving the vegetables. Bring juices to a simmer.

Add dried apricots and simmer until plump. Remove apricots with slotted spoon and reserve for garnish.

Place reserved vegetables in food processor and puree. Add puree to marinated juices. Blend cornstarch with cream and whisk into juices for gravy. Heat, stirring constantly, until thickened.

Slice meat thinly, garnish with apricots and serve with gravy.

About the Author

After twenty years of city living, life changed drastically for Carolyne Aarsen when she married and moved with her husband to a farm two hours away from the nearest mall. Neerlandia, the Canadian hamlet where they went to church and shopped, was so far from New York City, the hub of publishing, that her "someday" plans of writing a book seemed to belong to another world.

The dream wouldn't die, however, and while raising four of their own children and numerous foster children, Carolyne took a writing correspondence course. From that experience came a weekly column that ran for nine years in a number of northern Alberta newspapers. More writing courses and conferences finally led to her attaining her dream of publication.

She has published more than a dozen books that have combined her love of story with her love of the Lord. Carolyne is thankful that her writing permits her to show how God's extraordinary power can shape and change the lives of ordinary people.

Please visit www.carolyneaarsen.com and send her an e-mail if you have the time.